用搭配詞
英文變簡單

黃凱莉◎著

open to　　doubt

晨星出版

Preface 前言

出版的動機

學生最常問我的不是這個單字怎麼唸，而是為什麼我們要學英文！從他們憤怒不解的語氣中，我能體會到他們真的不懂全世界學生為什麼要學英文？為何要堅持說英文？其實答案很明顯，因為全球化的關係，英文已被當作外交、貿易、工業技術、尖端科學及國際化文明的通用語。

雖然中文擁有廣大使用人口，嘿嘿！英文使用的地區卻較普及，會中文很厲害，但要出國旅遊唸書時可無用武之地，看看那全球十大名校排行榜都在使用英文的英美國家，就算你有愛因斯坦的頭腦，不會英文，你發現了宇宙的秘密要說給誰聽？

本書搭配語就是根據自己在學習英文的路上發現到大家的學習障礙，而導致現實生活中工作或就學中產生的溝通或就業瓶頸，如果你在台灣學了英文超過 15 年，還無法應付即席英文自我介紹 3 分鐘或英文簡報，或是有一樣的以下煩惱，那本書絕對可以幫助你：

煩惱 1：學了一個單字，卻不知道要怎麼用或當這單字後連接不同介系詞時，慌了。
舉例：get 有得到或理解的意思，I got a present on my birthday.（我生日時得到一個禮物。）Don't get me wrong!（別誤會我的意思。）但是如果後面加了不同介系詞，意思大不同！I finally got over the sore throat!（我喉嚨痛終於好了！）Let me get back to you, your voice is breaking up!（讓我重打給你，你聲音斷斷續續的。）She is so mean. She is trying to get back at her colleague at the meeting.（她好壞，她在開會中公報私仇。）

煩惱 2：覺得閱讀一篇用正式複雜句子寫的學術報告、正式官方書信或英文報紙標題或時事專欄評論有困難。

煩惱 3：接觸到跟你英文發音或口音不一樣的交談者時，無法適應溝通

煩惱 4：只認得文章上的單字或句型，但卻無法用口語表達或解釋，也無法寫出自己的想法意見。

煩惱 5：對於開門 / 開店 / 開支票 / 啟動開關 / 節目開演，習慣一律用 open 表示。

本書架構 6 大特色

★單元精選單字：本書有 82 個單元，每一單元皆是精心設計超實用的生活主題，每單元中，精選大家之前都學過的，跟主題息息相關的單字，不用再另外背單字，能把重要的關鍵字應用在真實情境，學的精巧是重點。

★★英文解釋定義：英文要好，必殺技是能用簡單的英文解釋困難的英文單字或想法，本書針對自修者特別設計，英文解釋能力可當作口語訓練，會無礙的用英文讓人理解你的想法的人，條條大路通羅馬。

★★★常用搭配語公式表格：只會單字沒用，知道單字前後通常搭配一起的人才是厲害角色，作者觀察到台灣的英文學習者，大部分還在英文海裡沉浮，拼命求生的結果，想像力，表達力和英文修辭能力都很缺乏，本書的單字除了讓你溫故知新，工作生活上需要靈感時可參考使用搭配語，你將會發現一個單字加上搭配語可以開啟你無限想像。

★★★★實用例句：延續單字相關片語，特別加碼，正確使用相關介系詞讓你的英文更上一層樓，提升英文應用能力。

★★★★★情境表達套用語：所設計的生活化實際萬用句，遇到相似狀況可以直接套用，培養說英文的習慣。

★★★★★★有聲示範檔 QR code 無痛學習，躺著聽學道地自然語氣發音，讓你說一口令人印象深刻的漂亮英文。

每個單元配置 QR code 供掃描下載音檔，若不便用手機下載者，請輸入下網址，進入播放頁面後，按右鍵選擇「另存新檔」，即可存取 mp3 檔案。
音檔下載網址：http://epaper.morningstar.com.tw/mp3/0103354/01.mp3

請依單元編號 key 入下載，例如：02、03、04…依此類推

CONTENTS

Unit 1

Agreeing & Disagreeing
同意和意見不一致

Bone is the best.
骨頭最好吃！

No, fish is!
魚最好吃！

Betty and Sally disagree on almost everything !
貝蒂和莎莉常常意見不合！

agree (verb) 同意

定義 to share opinion, decide to say yes

常用搭配語 adv + agree

absolutely		完全同意
completely		完全同意
totally		完全同意
heartily		衷心地同意
wholeheartedly	agree	全心全意地同意
entirely		完全同意
strongly		強烈地同意
generally		大致上同意
provisionally		暫時地同意

tacitly	**agree**	有默契地同意
unanimously		一致地同意

📑 **實用例句** ・・・・・・・・・・・・・・・・・・・・・・・・・・・・・・・・・・・・・・

be mutually agreed on the proposal 互相地同意

After a few hours of meeting, they mutually agree on the proposal.

經過幾個小時的開會，他們互相同意了這個提案。

disagree (verb) 意見不合 / 不一致

定義 　to have different opinions with others, to fail to agree, to give a negative response

常用搭配語 　adv + disagree

totally	**disagree**	完全不同意
strongly		強烈不同意
completely		完全不同意
utterly		非常不同意
emotionally		情緒上不同意

📑 **實用例句** ・・・・・・・・・・・・・・・・・・・・・・・・・・・・・・・・・・・・・・

disagree on 對某事不同意

Betty and Sally disagree on almost everything!

貝蒂和莎莉常常意見不合！

communicate (verb) 溝通

定義 　to share opinion, decide to say yes

常用搭配語 　adv + communicate

effectively	**communicate**	有效地溝通
easily		簡單地溝通
directly		直接地溝通
clandestinely		暗中秘密地溝通
constantly		持續地溝通

實用例句 ·

to communicate well with people 與人溝通

Due to the globalization, we all have to communicate with our foreign clients in English.

由於全球化的關係，我們都得用英文跟我們的國外客戶溝通。

reconsider (verb) 重新考慮

定義　think again, think seriously

常用搭配語　adv + reconsider

contemplatively	reconsider	仔細地重新考慮
hastily		快速地重新考慮

實用例句 ·

reconsider the opportunity of 重新考慮某機會

I 'd better reconsider the opportunity of working overseas.

我最好重新考慮出國工作的機會。

convince (verb) 說服

定義　to make someone believe something is true. make someone agree to do something

常用搭配語　adv + convince

thoroughly	convinced	完全地被說服
firmly		毫不含糊地被說服
deeply		強烈地被說服
irresistibly		無法抗拒地被說服
theoretically		理論上被說服

實用例句 ·

become convinced 覺得

He became convinced that something is going odd!

他發覺事情要不妙了！

negotiation (noun) 談判 / 協商

定義 ➤ a serious conversation between people who are trying to reach an agreement

常用搭配語 ➤ adj + negotiation

bilateral		雙方的協商
difficult		困難的協商
lengthy	**negotiation**	冗長的談判
protracted		拖延時間的談判
behind-the-scene		幕後私下的協商
secret		秘密的協商

🗂 實用例句 ·

conduct negotiation with someone 與某人進行談判
We have been conducting the negotiation with one of our foreign affiliates since this morning.
我們從今早就一直跟其中一家海外加盟公司進行協商。

🔑 Key Expression
情境表達套用語

become a major disagreement between 對……變成主要導火線
Money has become a major disagreement between many couples.
金錢財務已成為夫妻之間常見的導火線。

Unit 2 | **Agriculture**
농업 — 農業

Overusing pesticides is more than likely to jeopardize our environment.
過度使用殺蟲劑一定會危害我們的環境。

grow (verb) 生長

定義 ➤ making more and more, increase, develop

常用搭配語 ➤ adv + grow

abundantly		豐富地生長
abnormally		不正常地生長
malignantly	grow	惡性地生長
tropically		熱帶環境地生長
vernally		春天蓬勃地生長
spiritually		精神上地成長

grow vegetable 種蔬菜

Have you ever thought about growing vegetables at your home？
你有曾經想過在家自己種蔬菜嗎？

harvest (noun) 收成

定義 ➤ reward, crop , product

常用搭配語 ➤ adj + harvest

terrible		糟糕的收成
abundant		大量的收成
poor	**harvest**	少的可憐的收成
rich		豐富的收成
fair		美好的收成

verb + harvest

celebrate		慶祝收成
get in	**harvest**	收割收成
house		貯藏收成

harvest + verb

	repays	收成得到回報
harvest	satisfies	收成滿足了

實用例句 ‧‧

poor harvest 收成慘淡

The fickle weather usually resulted in poor harvest for local fruit growers in Taiwan.
台灣多變的天氣通常造成當地果農的收成慘淡。

pesticide (noun) 殺蟲劑

定義 ▶ a chemical agent that is used to kill animals or insects

常用搭配語 ▶ adj + pesticide

hazardous		有害的殺蟲劑
banned	**pesticide**	被禁用的殺蟲劑
approved		准許使用的殺蟲劑

pesticide + noun

	use	殺蟲劑使用
pesticide	residues	殺蟲劑殘留
	contamination / pollution	殺蟲劑汙染

◈ 實用例句 ···

overusing pesticides 過度使用殺蟲劑

Overusing pesticides is more than likely to jeopardize our environment.
過度使用殺蟲劑一定會危害我們的環境。

fertilizer (noun) 肥料

定義 ▶ a natural or chemical substance that is added in the soil to help the plants grow better

常用搭配語 ▶ verb + fertilizer

advocate		提倡肥料
apply	**fertilizer**	使用肥料
purchase		購買肥料
replenish		重新補充肥料

◈ 實用例句 ···

all-natural fertilizer 全天然肥料

There are more and more farmers making all-natural fertilizer in their backyard.
有愈多愈來的農夫在自己的後院自製全天然肥料。

produce (noun) 農產品

定義 → fresh fruits and vegetables

常用搭配語 → adj + produce

organic		有機農產品
farm		農場農產品
seasonal	produce	季節性農產品
fresh		新鮮農產品
local		當地農產品

實用例句

a wide range of produce 各式各樣的農產品
There is a wide range of produce on display in the farmer's market.
在農夫市集裡有各式各樣的農產品展示。

Key Expression
情境表達套用語

a wild card 變數
Weather plays as a wild card to fruit harvest for local farmers.
天氣對當地農夫的水果收成一直扮演著變數的角色。

Unit 3 | **Animals & Pets**
動物和寵物

> What's the matter with you?
> 你怎麼了，貓奴。

I have been looking into some ways to get rid of fleas on my pet naturally.
我一直在找如何天然的去除我寵物身上的跳蚤。

必學！外國人習慣用的動物特殊計量詞

a flock of	birds	一群鳥
a herd of	sheep / elephants	一群羊 / 象群
a litter of	puppies / kittens	一窩小狗小貓
a pack of	wolves / wild dogs	一群狼 / 野狗
a pod of	whales	一小群鯨魚
a pride of	lions	一群獅子
a plague of	locusts	一大群蝗蟲
a school of	fish	一群魚
a swarm of	bees / ants	一群蜜蜂螞蟻
a troop of	monkeys	一群猴子

adopt (verb) 領養 / 接受

定義 → to choose someone or something

常用搭配語 → adj + adopt

legally		合法地領養
formally	**adopt**	正式地領養
officially		正式地領養

實用例句 ···

finally adopted 終於被接受

My proposal is finally adopted by the team!

我的提案終於被團隊接受了！

pet (noun) 寵物

定義 → an animal kept for companionship

常用搭配語 → idiom- 慣用語

pet peeve 無傷大雅的小毛病，在別人眼中看來很奇怪，比如說不喜歡被超車或被按喇叭，如果別人這樣做，你就會抓狂生氣。

adj + pet

domestic		家庭寵物
family		家庭寵物
household	**pet**	家庭寵物
lovely		可愛寵物
adoptable		可領養的寵物

實用例句 ···

get rid of fleas on my pet 去除我寵物身上的跳蚤

I have been looking into some ways to get rid of fleas on my pet naturally.

我一直在找如何天然的去除我寵物身上的跳蚤。

breed (noun) 品種

定義 ▸ type of animal

常用搭配語 ▸ adj + breed

new		新品種
rare		稀有品種
hardy	**breed**	吃苦耐勞的品種
ancient		古老品種
pure-blooded		純血統的品種

◈ 實用例句 ······················

what breed 什麼品種

Your dog looks fantastic, what breed is it？

你的狗看起來棒透了！它是什麼品種啊？

protect (verb) 保護

定義 ▸ to keep someone or something from being hurt / harmed

常用搭配語 ▸ adj + protect

fully		完全地保護
successfully		成功地保護
parentally	**protect**	向雙親一樣地保護
properly		妥善地保護
carefully		仔細地保護

◈ 實用例句 ······················

protect women 保護女性

This forum is to protect women against violence.

這個園地是為了保護女性免受暴力。

accompany (verb) 陪伴

定義	to be, go, or stay with

常用搭配語	adj + accompany

delightedly		開心地陪伴
unhappily	**accompany**	不高興地陪伴
spiritually		精神上地陪伴

實用例句

was accompanied by 由……陪伴

He went to the event and was accompanied by his wife.

他由妻子陪伴出席了那個宴會。

Key Expression
情境表達套用語

animal lovers 愛動物的人

She is such an animal lover! She keeps 5 cats and 4 dogs.

她真是個動物愛好者！她養了五隻貓和四隻狗。

Unit 4

Arts & Crafts
藝術和手工藝

Wow, I get a good shot.
哇！我拍了一張好照片！

Wedding photography business is growing fast in Taiwan.
結婚攝影的生意在台灣快速發展中。

display (noun) 展示

定義 ── to show the arrangement of something so people can see it

常用搭配語 ── adj + display

public		公開展示
permanent		永久展示
static	display	靜態展示
temporary		臨時展示

📚 實用例句 ·

floral display 花卉展示
The floral display in the opening is quite beautiful.
開幕式的花卉展示相當漂亮。

sketch (noun) 草稿 / 速寫

定義 ▶ quick drawing

常用搭配語 ▶ adj + sketch

quick		快速的草稿
rough	sketch	大約的速寫
preliminary		初步的略圖
charcoal		炭筆素描

實用例句

do sketch of 畫……的素描
I did some sketches of the trees in my leisure time.
我空閒時有畫了些樹木的素描寫生。

exhibit (noun) 展覽

定義 ▶ to show an object or collection for people

常用搭配語 ▶ adj + exhibit

art		藝術展覽
educational		教育展覽
admirable	exhibit	令人激賞的展覽
startling		令人吃驚的展覽
representative		代表性的展覽

實用例句

the latest sculpture exhibit 最新的雕塑展
Have you seen the latest sculpture exhibit in town?
市區裡最新的雕塑展你去看了沒？

painting (noun) 畫

定義 ▶ drawing, the picture that is drawn and painted

常用搭配語 ▶ adj + painting

portrait		人物畫
contemporary	**painting**	現代畫
delicate		精美的畫
priceless		無價的畫

實用例句 ·

mysterious painting 神祕之畫

The Mona Lisa is a mysterious painting that caught everyone's attention.

蒙娜麗莎是一幅吸引眾人目光的神祕之畫。

capture (verb) 捕捉

定義 to catch, get control of something

常用搭配語 adv + capture

perfectly		完美地捕捉
skillfully	**capture**	有技巧地捕捉
finally		最後補捉
previously		事先地捕捉

實用例句 ·

brilliantly captured 高明地捕捉

This painting brilliantly captured the girl's emotion.

這幅畫高明地捕捉到了少女的情感。

Key Expression
情境表達套用語

take artistic license 不按牌理出牌 / 不拘泥於傳統規則的做法

He is famous for taking artistic license in the films he made.

他製作的電影以顛覆傳統的風格聞名。

Unit 5 | **Blames**
責怪

Don't tell her anything. She is a gossip.
不要告訴她任何事，她超會八卦的。

Bring it on, I don't care.
放馬過來，我才不在乎呢！

I would have to stifle my anger when I learned that Jenny was talking behind my back.
當我知道珍妮在我背後說我壞話，我只得按兵不動。

blame (verb) 責怪

定義 say or think someone or something happened is wrong

常用搭配語 blame + verb

unfairly		不公平地責怪
unthinkingly	**blame**	不加思考地責怪
narrow-mindedly		心胸狹隘地責怪
completely		一昧地責怪

📚 實用例句 ∙∙∙∙∙∙∙∙∙∙∙∙∙∙∙∙∙∙∙∙∙∙∙∙∙∙∙∙∙∙∙∙∙∙∙∙∙∙

blaming the economic downturn for 怪在經濟不景氣頭上

There are more and more companies now blaming the economic downturn for their poor sales.

有愈來愈多的公司把業績不良怪在經濟不景氣頭上。

complaint (noun) 抱怨

| 定義 | acting of complaining |

| 常用搭配語 | adj + complaint |

consumer / customer		顧客抱怨
distressing		令人痛苦的抱怨
formal	**complaint**	正式報怨
frequent		經常性的抱怨
troublesome		令人討厭的抱怨

◈ 實用例句 ·

lodge a customer complaint 提出客訴
I need to lodge a customer complaint to your store manager immediately.
我需要立刻找你們的店經理提出客訴。

stifle (verb) 忍住

| 定義 | to stop from doing something |

| 常用搭配語 | stifle + noun |

	anger	忍住怒氣
stifle	laughter	忍住不笑
	sorrow	忍住悲傷

◈ 實用例句 ·

stifle my anger 按兵不動
I would have to stifle my anger when I learned that Jenny was talking behind my back.
當我知道珍妮在我背後說我壞話，我只得按兵不動。

excuse (noun) 藉口

| 定義 | some reasons you give to explain your mistakes or bad things |

| 常用搭配語 | adj + excuse |

apparent		明顯的藉口
flimsy	**excuse**	站不住腳的藉口
pathetic		可悲的藉口
reasonable		合理的藉口

◈ 實用例句 ···

feeble excuse 薄弱的理由

He made a feeble excuse on not doing his homework.

他編了一個薄弱的沒做回家作業的理由。

splutter (verb) 嘟囔聲

> **定義** ▸ to say something in short and confused words

> **常用搭配語** ▸ splutter + noun

splutter	noise	發出氣急敗壞的聲音

◈ 實用例句 ···

coughing and spluttering 上氣不接下氣

He rushed to the office, coughing and spluttering.

他衝到辦公室，上氣不接下氣的樣子。

🔑 Key Expression
情境表達套用語

call someone down 責罵

It was embarassing when teacher called me down in front of everyone.

老師當著大家的面罵我一頓，真的讓我很窘。

Unit 6

Beginning & Ending
開始和結束

We can't go any further. It is a dead end.
這是死路一條,我們不能再往前了!

begin (verb) 開始

| 定義 | to start something |

| 常用搭配語 | verb + begin |

be ready to	begin	準備要開始
be scheduled to		預計要開始

adv + begin

hesitatingly	begin	猶豫地開始
clumsily		笨手笨腳地開始
ostensibly		表面上地開始

◇ 實用例句 ·

is scheduled to begin 預計要開始

This project is scheduled to begin in coming June.
這個專案預計在今年六月開始。

end (noun) 結束 / 終點

| 定義 | the furthest part of something |

| 常用搭配語 | adj + end |

dead	**end**	死路

verb + end

reach		到達終點
pray for	**end**	祈禱快結束
progress toward		向結果邁進

實用例句 •

It is a dead end. 這是死路一條
We can't go any further. It is a dead end.
這是死路一條，我們不能再往前了。

initiate (verb) 開始

| 定義 | to begin, introduce |

| 常用搭配語 | adj + initiate |

ceremoniously		拘泥地開始
dramatically	**initiate**	戲劇性地開始
formally		正式地開始

實用例句 •

initiated shortly 將會開始
The ceremony will be formally initiated shortly.
典禮不久將會正式開始。

reach (verb) 到達

| 定義 | arrive at a place or condition |

| 常用搭配語 | adv + reach |

automatically		自動地到達
finally	**reach**	終於到達 .
promptly		快速地到達

◈ 實用例句

within easy reach of 四通八達
My house is located within easy reach of all stores.
我家位置到所有商店都很方便。

process (noun) 過程

| 定義 | a series of actions to produce something |

| 常用搭配語 | adj + process |

beautifying		美化的過程
lengthy		漫長的過程
chemical	**process**	化學的過程
aging		老化的過程

◈ 實用例句

tedious process 漫長乏味的過程
I hate that I have to go through that tedious process to apply for files each time.
我很討厭每次申請文件都要經過漫長乏味的過程。

🔑 Key Expression
情境表達套用語

start from scratch 從頭開始
I started this project from scratch, no one knows it better than I do.
這個專案我從頭就有參與，沒有人比我更了解這個案子。

Unit 7

Beauty & Fashion
美麗和時尚

> Oh dear,What should I wear for today?
> 討厭，今天該穿什麼好呢？

Women always need one more clothes in their wardrobe.
女人衣櫃裡總需要再多一件衣服。

brand (noun) 品牌

定義 ▶ a mark that is made by a particular company

常用搭配語 ▶ adj + brand

leading		領導品牌
famous		著名品牌
well-known	**brand**	知名品牌
own		自家品牌

🗂 實用例句 ・・・・・・・・・・・・・・・・・・・・・・・・・・・・・・・・・・・

own brand 自家品牌

We can see lots of supermarkets now selling their own brand products.
我們可以看到很多超市都在銷售自家品牌了。

style (noun) 風格

定義 a way of showing or doing things

常用搭配語 adj + style

different		不同的風格
latest		最新的風格
old-fashioned		老掉牙的風格
original	style	原創風格
casual		休閒風格
inimitable		無可仿效的風格

實用例句 ⋯⋯⋯⋯⋯⋯⋯⋯⋯⋯⋯⋯⋯⋯⋯⋯⋯⋯⋯⋯⋯

oozed style 散發出風格

His own-designed house just oozed style. Fantastic!

他自己設計的房子就是散發出風格，讚！！

wardrobe (noun) 衣櫥

定義 a closet / room for clothes

常用搭配語 adj + wardrobe

built-in		一體成型的衣櫥
double	wardrobe	雙人衣櫥
walk-in		大到人走得進去的衣櫥

實用例句 ⋯⋯⋯⋯⋯⋯⋯⋯⋯⋯⋯⋯⋯⋯⋯⋯⋯⋯⋯⋯⋯

wardrobe 衣櫃

Women always need one more clothes in their wardrobe.

女人衣櫃裡總需要再多一件衣服。

accessory (noun) 飾品

定義 something added to something make it more beautiful or attractive

常用搭配語 adj + accessory

fashionable		流行飾品
colorful		色彩繽紛的飾品
impressive	**accessory**	令人印象深刻的飾品
disposable		用過即可丟的飾品
clothing		服裝配件

🗂 實用例句 ··

fashionable accessories 流行飾品

She is a shopkeeper of fashionable accessories.

她是一家流行飾品店的老闆。

collection (noun) 收集

定義 something gathered together to show a hobby or study

常用搭配語 adj + collection

unique		獨一無二的收集
diverse		多樣化的收集
stunning	**collection**	令人驚嘆的收集
private		私人收集
random		隨機收集

🗂 實用例句 ··

stamp collection 郵票收集

My stamp collection has gradually become valuable.

我收藏的郵票越來越有價值了。

Key Expression
情境表達套用語

out of fashion 過時

I don't like the dress that my mom bought me last week. It is so out of fashion.

我不喜歡上星期我媽買給我那件洋裝，好土喔！

Unit 8

Business
商業

It is hard to differentiate this one from the other.
這兩個很難分辨有什麼不一樣。

---

deal (noun) 交易

定義 ► the act of trade, business

常用搭配語 ► adj + deal

neighborly		親切的交易
legitimate	**deal**	正當的交易
make-to-order		客製化的交易
the last-minute		最後一刻的交易

實用例句 ·····························

sponsorship deal 贊助
The sexual scandal scuppered his sponsorship deal.
性醜聞讓他的贊助泡湯了。

boom (noun) 起飛 / 好轉

定義 ► a sudden increase of something

常用搭配語 ► adj / n + boom

economic		經濟起飛
periodic		周期性的好轉
unprecedented	**boom**	前所未有的好轉
property		房地產好轉
investment		投資好轉

◈ 實用例句 ·····················

market boomed 市場蓬勃發展

The mobile phone market boomed in China after free trade policy.

在自由貿易政策下，大陸手機市場蓬勃發展。

industry (noun) 行業

定義 ► a group of businesses that provide certain services

常用搭配語 ► adj + industry

thriving		欣欣向榮的行業
major		主要行業
declining		衰敗的行業
labor-intensive	**industry**	勞力密集的行業
domestic		國內工業
government-owned		國營行業
privatized		民營行業

local tourist industry 當地觀光業

They worry about that vanishing natural landscape might damage the local tourist industry.

他們擔心消失的天然景觀可能會對當地觀光業造成損失。

commodity (noun) 商品

定義　product, material

常用搭配語　adj + commodity

rare		稀有的商品
perishable		生鮮產品
marketable	**commodity**	值得賣的商品
primary		主要的商品
export		出口的商品
agricultural		農業的商品

實用例句 ・・

Imported commodities 進口商品

Imported commodities are usually tagged with higher price than local ones.

進口商品通常售價會比本地商品高。

economize (verb) 節約 / 緊縮開支

定義　to try to save money

常用搭配語　economize + on

economize	on	節約

實用例句 ・・

economize on water 節約用水

People have learned to economize on water during the critical period of drought.
大家都知道在極端乾旱時期要節約用水。

differentiate (verb) 區分

定義 ➤ to be able to tell the difference between the two

常用搭配語 ➤ be + adj + to + differentiate

be important to		很重要去區分
be easy to	**differentiate**	很容易去區分
be difficult to		很困難去區分
be possible to		有可能去區分

實用例句

differentiate one from the other 分辨有什麼不一樣
It is hard to differentiate this one from the other.
這兩個很難分辨有什麼不一樣。

Key Expression
情境表達套用語

USP (Unique Selling Point) 產品獨特賣點
The product with USP will sell itself.
有賣點的產品會自己行銷。

Unit 9

Causes & Effects
因和果

Mary is also my friend. Are you jealous?
瑪麗也是我的朋友，你幹嘛吃醋？

Stop talking to Mary. She is my girl friend
不准你和瑪麗說話，她是我的女朋友。

That's the reason why they argued!
這就是他們爭吵的原因！

reason (noun) 理由 / 原因

| 定義 | explanation of something |

常用搭配語 ▶ adj + reason

for no apparent		沒有明顯的理由
understandable		可以理解的原因
personal	**reason**	個人原因
underlying		根本原因
humanitarian		人道理由

◇ 實用例句 ·······················

underlying reason 根本原因

I think the underlying reason of the change of her heart will become more clearer when we meet her in person.
我認為跟她親自碰面，才會比較了解她改變主意的根本原因。

personal reason 個人原因
Jaclyn asked for 3 day's leave on personal reason.
Jaclyn 因個人因素請了 3 天的假。

reciprocate (verb) 回報

定義　　　to do something for someone who has done the same thing to you.

常用搭配語　　　reciporcate + noun

reciprocate	compliment	回報讚美
	favor	回報恩惠
	kindness	回報好意
	hospitality	回報款待

實用例句

reciprocated the hospitality 回報款待之意
Tom kindly reciprocated the hospitality by dropping us off in the airport.
湯姆好心地載我們到機場回報款待之意。

reciprocate favor 回報恩惠
I reciprocated the favor by gifting a jar of honey to my neighbor, who watered my plants when I was out of town.
我送了一罐蜂蜜給我鄰居回報他在我出遠門時幫我澆花的恩情。

impact (noun) 衝擊

定義　　　to have a big or strong effect on something or someone

常用搭配語　　　adj + impact

huge		巨大的衝擊
overall		全面的衝擊
negligible	**impact**	無關緊要的衝擊
far-reaching		深遠的衝擊
serious		嚴重的衝擊

📚 實用例句 ···

direct impact 直接的衝擊

The cyber bookstore has made a direct impact on physical bookstores.

虛擬網路書店對實體書店已造成了直接的衝擊。

consequence (noun) 後果

定義 something happened as a result

常用搭配語 adj + consequence

no great		沒有很大的後果
inevitable		不可避免的後果
unintended	**consequence**	非計畫中的後果
economic		經濟的後果

📚 實用例句 ···

economic consequence 經濟後果

People in Iraq are suffering the economic consequence of the war.

伊拉克人民飽受戰爭帶來的經濟後果。

inevitable consequence 不可避免的後果

Drunk and drive might lead to inevitable consequence.

酒後駕車可能會導致不可避免的後果。

influence (noun) 影響

| 定義 | something or someone change or affect someone or something |

| 常用搭配語 | prep + influence |

under	the influence	在……影響下

adj + influence

profound		意義重大的影響
overwhelming		壓倒性的影響
wide	influence	廣泛的影響
crucial		決定性的影響

實用例句

overwhelming influence 壓倒性的影響力
His speech had an overwhelming influence on people.
他的演講對眾人有壓倒性的影響力。

profound influence 意義深遠的影響
The Italian Renaissance in the 16th century has a profound influence on the art world.
16 世紀的義大利文藝復興對藝術史產生了意義深遠的影響。

Key Expression
情境表達套用語

get back at someone 報復 / 公報私仇
She got back at me during the meeting.
她在會議室對我公報私仇。

Certainty & Uncertainty
確定與不確定

I didn't mean that.
我不是故意的。

Let me assure you that this won't happen again.
我可以向你擔保這不會再發生。

certain (adjective) 確定

定義 ▶ to be sure about something with no doubt

常用搭配語 ▶ adv + certain

absolutely		絕對確定
by no means	**certain**	絕對不可能
almost		幾乎確定

◇ 實用例句 ·

not quite certain 不太確定

I am not quite certain that I will get the job.
我並不太確定我會得到那個工作。

doubt (noun) 懷疑

定義 ▸ to be unsure about something

常用搭配語 ▸ verb + doubt

raise		提出懷疑
feel		感覺懷疑
dispel		清除懷疑
cast	doubt	拋出懷疑
throw into		使人懷疑
open to		值得懷疑

◈ 實用例句 ···

cast doubt 受到質疑

Her constantly absent from work cast doubts on her ability at work.
她一直沒來上班讓她的工作能力受到質疑。

reconfirm (verb) 再次確認

定義 ▸ to make sure of something again

常用搭配語 ▸ adv + reconfirm

amply		詳細地再次確認
speedily	reconfirm	快速地再次確認
explicitly		明確地再次確認

◈ 實用例句 ···

explicitly reconfirmed the order 明確地再次確認訂單

She explicitly reconfirmed the order with an overseas client on the phone.
她在電話裡跟海外客戶明確地再次確認訂單。

assure (verb) assured (adj) 放心

定義 ▶ be sure to happen

常用搭配語 ▶ verb + assured

rest		放心
look	**assured**	看起來確定
seem		似乎肯定

adv + assured

absolutely	**assured**	確信

實用例句 •

Let me assure you. 我可以擔保

Let me assure you that this won't happen again.

我可以向你擔保這不會再發生。

🔑 Key Expression
情境表達套用語

flimsy excuse 跛腳的藉口

She just gave a flimsy excuse for her absence from work.

她剛為自己沒來上班編了一個跛腳的藉口。

Chance & Luck
僥倖和運氣

dodged the bullet
九死一生

He dodged the bullet, but he survived.
他經歷了九死一生，但他存活下來了。

opportunity (noun) 機會

定義 ▶ chance, a situation that something can be done

常用搭配語 ▶ adj + opportunity

every		每一個機會
golden		黃金機會
wonderful		絕佳機會
once-in-a-life-time	opportunity	一生一次的機會
photo		拍照的機會 (通常是跟名人)
equal		一律平等

實用例句 ·······································

golden opportunity 黃金機會

It is a golden opportunity to invest now.

現在可是投資的黃金機會。

random (adj) 隨機

定義 something chosen without a method or pattern

常用搭配語 adv + random

completely		完全地隨機
apparently		明顯隨地機
seemingly	random	似乎是隨機
entirely		完全地隨機
purely		純粹是隨機

實用例句 ·······································

at random 隨機

The hostess just picked random audience from the crowd to the stage.

女主持人就隨機挑了幾個觀眾上台。

choose (verb) 選擇

定義 to decide something or someone you want

常用搭配語 adv + choose

mistakenly		錯誤地選擇
sympathetically		有同情心地選擇
arbitrarily	choose	任意地選擇
finally		最後地選擇

pick and choose 挑三揀四

There is no time to pick and choose. we need to catch the bus now!

沒時間挑三揀四了！我們現在要去趕公車了。

coincidence (noun) 巧合

定義 ➤ happening at the same time

常用搭配語 ➤ adj + conincidence

strange		奇怪的巧合
mere		僅僅是巧合
unexpected	**coincidence**	意想不到的巧合
occasional		偶爾發生的巧合

🐚 **實用例句** ••

By strange coincidence 因為奇怪的巧合

By strange coincidence, I ran into her several times in the office.

因為奇怪的巧合，我在辦公室碰到她好幾次。

unfortunate (adj) 不幸的

定義 ➤ unlucky, having bad luck

常用搭配語 ➤ unfortunate + noun

	event	不幸的事件
	young man	不幸的年輕人
unfortunate	choice of words	出言不遜
	decision	悲慘的決定
	lack of taste	不幸的缺乏品味

adv + unfortunate

extremely		極端地不幸
rather	**unfortunate**	相當地不幸
slightly		稍微小小地不幸

實用例句

It is unfortunate 很不幸的
It is unfortunate that she lost her entire family in a highway car crash.
她很不幸的在一場高速公路車禍中失去她所有家人。

unfortunate lack of taste 不幸的缺乏品味
Due to unfortunate lack of taste, she is called as "fashion disaster."
由於不幸的缺乏品味，人人叫她「時尚災難」。

Key Expression
情境表達套用語

dodge the bullet 九死一生
He dodged the bullet , but he survived.
他經歷了九死一生，但他存活下來了。

Changes

改變

She openly criticized the idea of raising taxes.
她公開地批判加稅的想法。

---

criticize (verb) 批判

定義 ▸ to talk about something with problems or faults

常用搭配語 ▸ adv +criticize

openly		公開地批判
sharply	**criticize**	嚴厲地批判
constantly		持續地批判

◇ 實用例句 ‧‧‧‧‧‧‧‧‧‧‧‧‧‧‧‧‧‧‧‧‧‧‧‧‧‧‧‧‧‧‧‧‧‧‧‧‧

openly criticize 公開地批判

She openly criticized the idea of raising taxes.
她公開地批判加稅的想法。

importonate (adj) 糾纏

| 定義 | to keep making troublesome requests |

| 常用搭配語 | adv + importunate |

endlessly		永無止盡地糾纏
provokingly	importunate	令人生氣地糾纏
obnoxiously		惹人厭地糾纏

importunate + noun

	crowd	糾纏不休的群眾
importunate	beggar	陰魂不散的乞丐
	lover	糾纏不清的愛人

◇ 實用例句 ·····································

increasingly importunate 變本加厲地

He has been increasingly importunate to harass me for the past few months.

過去這幾個月來，他一直變本加厲地騷擾我。

debunk (verb) 揭露 / 揭穿

| 定義 | to show something (such as a story, idea, theory) is not true |

| 常用搭配語 | adv + debunk |

assiduously	debunk	努力不懈地揭露
easily		輕而易舉地揭穿

◇ 實用例句 ·····································

assiduously debunked 毫不懈怠地揭穿

The reporter assiduously debunked a long-held misconception every week on his column.

這個記者每星期毫不懈怠地在他的專欄上揭穿深植人心的錯誤觀念。

conflict (noun) 衝突

| 定義 | the opposition or difference between ideas and feelings |

major		主要的衝突
serious		嚴重的衝突
increasing	**conflict**	增加的衝突
constant		持續的衝突
cultural		文化的衝突

實用例句 ···

in constant conflict with 衝突不斷

She has been in constant conflict with her family since she was a teenager.

她從青少年時就一直跟她的家庭衝突不斷。

transform 變化

定義 ▶ someone or something changed completely

常用搭配語 ▶ adv + transform

dramatically		戲劇化地變化
gradually	**transform**	逐漸地變化
suddenly		突然地變化

實用例句 ···

transformed overnight 一夕之間轉好

Everybody knows that bad economy couldn't be transformed overnight.

大家都知道壞經濟不可能一夕之間轉好。

Key Expression
情境表達套用語

all of a sudden 突然

All of a sudden, we heard a piercing screaming.

突然我們聽到一聲刺耳的尖叫。

Unit 13 | **Choices & Decisions**
選擇和決定

We are on honeymoon.
蜜月中。

Just Married

2Y5

The newly wedded couple finally decided where to spend their honeymoon.
那對新婚夫妻終於決定要去哪度蜜月了。

decide (verb) 決定

定義 to choose from choices

常用搭配語 adv + decide

finally		終於決定
speedily	decide	很快地決定
wisely		明智地決定
discreetly		謹慎地決定

實用例句

finally decide 終於決定
The newly wedded couple finally decided where to spend their honeymoon.
那對新婚夫妻終於決定要去哪度蜜月了。

alternative (noun) 選擇 / 替代方案

定義 ➤ other choices or options for something

常用搭配語 ➤ adj + alternative

acceptable		可接受的替代方案
possible		可能的替代方案
practical	**alternative**	實際可行的選擇
suitable		合適的選擇
healthier		更健康的選擇

實用例句 ·

leave me no alternative but to call 讓我沒選擇的餘地只好……
You leave me no alternative but to call the police now!
你讓我沒選擇的餘地，我只好報警了。

acceptable alternative 可接受的替代方案
He proposed an acceptable alternative for my loss.
他提出了一個針對我的損失，還可以接受的替代方案。

select (verb) 選擇

定義 ➤ choose, determine the one you like

常用搭配語 ➤ adv + select

carefully		小心地選擇
deliberately		故意 (有意) 地選擇
randomly	**select**	隨機地選擇
personally		親自地選擇

實用例句 ·

personally select 親自地挑選
She personally selected the color that her boyfriend would like.
她親自地挑選了她男朋友會喜歡的顏色。

regret (verb) (noun) 後悔

定義 ▸ you feel sorry and unhappy about something you did or were unable to do

常用搭配語 ▸ adv + regret

deeply	regret	深深地後悔
immediately		立刻地後悔

adj + regret

the biggest		最大的後悔
deep		深切的後悔
real	regret	真正的後悔
bitter		令人痛苦的後悔
sincere		真誠的後悔

◈ **實用例句** ·

the biggest regret 最後悔的事
Dropping out of school was the biggest regret of my life.
中途輟學是我這輩子最後悔的事。

regretted immediately 立刻後悔
I regretted immediately after I made the call.
我打完電話後立刻後悔了！

tackle (verb) 處理

定義 ▸ deal with a problem or difficulty

常用搭配語 ▸ adv + tackle

properly		正確地處理
successfully		成功地處理
efficiently	tackle	有效地處理
directly		直接地解決

實用例句 ··

failed to tackle 無法處理
He failed to tackle the personnel issue in time.
他無法及時的處理這個人事問題。

directly tackle our problems 直接處理我們的問題
We are asked to contact manager to directly tackle our problems.
我們被要求跟主管聯絡，直接處理我們的問題。

Key Expression
情境表達套用語

added value 附加價值
This product has one more added value than the others.
這個產品比其他的多一個附加價值。

Clothes & Fashion

衣服穿著

I decked out for my birthday party.
我盛裝出席生日派對。

I lifted up my dress so I wouldn't get tripped by it.
我撩起禮服免得被絆倒了。

dress (noun) 服裝

定義 ➤ a piece of clothing to wear

常用搭配語 ➤ adj + dress

skimpy		清涼的 (布料很少) 服裝
slinky		緊身的服裝
loose-fitting	dress	寬鬆的服裝
ball		宴會服
ankle-length		腳踝長度的衣服
strapless		無肩帶服裝

實用例句 ···

lifted up my dress 撩起我的禮服
I lifted up my dress so I wouldn't get tripped by it.
我撩起禮服免得被絆倒了。

trend (noun) 趨勢

定義 ➤ the way of becoming more and more popular and fashionable

常用搭配語 ➤ adj + trend

growing		成長的趨勢
main		主要的趨勢
clear	**trend**	清楚的趨勢
downward		往下滑的趨勢

🔖 實用例句 ‧‧‧‧‧‧‧‧‧‧‧‧‧‧‧‧‧‧‧‧‧‧‧‧‧‧‧‧‧‧‧

downward trend 往下滑的趨勢
I am pretty worried about the current downward trend in sales.
我真的很擔心現在一直往下掉的業績。

fashion (noun) 時尚 / 流行

定義 ➤ the clothes or the things that are popular

常用搭配語 ➤ adj + fashion

female		女性時尚
street		街頭時尚
latest	**fashion**	最新流行
youth		青少年流行

🔖 實用例句 ‧‧‧‧‧‧‧‧‧‧‧‧‧‧‧‧‧‧‧‧‧‧‧‧‧‧‧‧‧‧‧

keep up with the latest fashion 跟上最新流行
It was kind of silly for her to spend a lot of money keeping up with the latest fashion.
她花了大把銀子跟上最新流行真是有點蠢。

design (noun) 設計

定義 ➤ to think or plan something should be made for certain use

常用搭配語 ➤ adj + design

graphic		平面設計
architectural	**design**	建築設計
interior		室內設計

實用例句 ···

graphic design 平面設計
She is specializing in graphic design.
她專精平面設計。

accessory (noun) 飾品

定義 something you add or wear to make yourself more attractive or beautiful

常用搭配語 adj + accessory

fashion		流行飾品
perfect		完美配件
useful	**accessory**	好用的配件
car		車用配件

實用例句 ···

prefect accessory 完美配件
Belts become the prefect accessory in this season.
皮帶在這一季變身為完美配件。

Key Expression
情境表達套用語

out of stock 沒庫存
Sorry, this size is currently out of stock.
真抱歉！這個尺寸現在沒庫存了。

Unit 15

Complaints
抱怨

They don't let me refund.
店員不讓我退貨。

Complaints

One of his duties is to properly deal with daily complaints from his store shoppers.
妥當地處理每天來自店裡顧客的客訴是他的工作職責之一。

complaint (noun) 抱怨

定義	→	something you say when you are unhappy with it

| 常用搭配語 | → | verb + complaint |

have		有抱怨
bring		帶來抱怨
file		提出抱怨
lodge	complaint	提出抱怨
receive		接到抱怨
deal with		處理抱怨
respond to		回應抱怨

◈ 實用例句 •

daily complaint 每天的客訴

One of his duties is to properly deal with daily complaints from his store shoppers.
妥當地處理每天來自店裡顧客的客訴是他的工作職責之一。

negotiate (verb) 協商

定義 ▶ to try to reach an agreement

常用搭配語 ▶ adv + negotiate

carefully		小心地協商
continually	**negotiate**	繼續地協商
successfully		成功地協商
directly		直接地協商

◈ 實用例句 ···

directly negotiate with 直接地協商
I have got to directly negotiate with our foreign client about price of bulk purchase.
我得要直接地跟國外客戶協商大量購買的價錢。

attitude (noun) 態度

定義 ▶ the way you think about a fact or state

常用搭配語 ▶ adj + attitude

right		正確的態度
wrong	**attitude**	錯誤的態度
carefree		自在的態度
conservative		保守的態度

◈ 實用例句 ···

take positive attitude 採取正面態度
I have decided to take positive attitude to this problem.
我已經決定要對這個問題採取正面態度。

handle (verb) 處理

定義 ▶ to act or manage something

carefully		小心地處理
carelessly	**handle**	漫不經心地處理
easily		容易地處理
properly		妥善地處理

實用例句 ●

handle with care 小心輕放

Please write the words " handle with care " with red marker on the sides of the container.

請用紅色馬克筆在箱子四周寫下「小心輕放」。

scream (noun) 尖叫

定義　　a loud and sharp noise

常用搭配語　　► verb+scream

give		發出尖叫
let out	**scream**	發出尖叫
hear		聽到尖叫

實用例句 ●

give scream 發出尖叫

The audience is giving exciting screams in the concert.

演唱會裡的觀眾發出興奮的尖叫。

Key Expression
情境表達套用語

raise your voice 提高音量

Don't raise your voice, you are scaring the children.

別那麼大聲，你嚇到小孩了。

Unit 16

Computer & Internet

電腦和網路

> I just love shopping from home.
> 我喜歡宅在家網購。

Many traditional stores found out getting clicks and bricks strategy is a great way to both serve and keep shoppers.

許多傳統商店已經發現打實體和網路店面策略，才能同時服務和留住消費者。

assemble (verb) 組裝

| 定義 | to meet together, to put every little part together |

| 常用搭配語 | adv + assemble |

fully		完全地組裝
quickly		快速地組裝
easily	assemble	容易地組裝
carefully		小心地組裝

📑 實用例句 ·····························

assemble in the auditorium 集聚在大禮堂

We are told to assemble in the auditorium for a speech.

我們被告知要去禮堂集合聽演講。

component (noun) 元件

定義 ▶ one factor or part to make one whole thing

常用搭配語 ▶ adj + component

basic		基本元件
crucial	**component**	關鍵性元件
major		主要元件
standard		標準元件

實用例句 ···

computer component supplier 電腦元件供應商
I used to work for the major computer component supplier in Taiwan 5 years ago.
我五年前曾經在台灣最大的一間電腦元件供應商工作過。

establish (verb) 成立

定義 ▶ to build, to begin, to set up

常用搭配語 ▶ adv + establish

newly		新成立
firmly	**establish**	堂堂成立
splendidly		華麗成立
officially		正式成立

實用例句 ···

splendidly establish 華麗成立
The main building was splendidly established during the economy boom.
這棟大樓在經濟起飛時華麗地落成了。

skill (noun) 技巧

定義 ▶ the ability from learning makes you can get something well done

常用搭配語 ▶ adj + skill

language		語言技巧
interpersonal	**skill**	人際關係技巧
basic		基本技巧
culinary		烹飪技巧

◇ 實用例句 ....

basic language skill 基本聽說讀寫

A mastery of basic language skill is required for this position.

勝任這個工作需要精通基本聽說讀寫。

output (noun) 生產

定義 something that is produced by a person or a machine

常用搭配語 adj + output

steady		穩定的生產
prolific	**output**	大量的生產
profitable		有利可圖的生產
excessive		生產過剩

◇ 實用例句 ....

metal output 金屬生產量

The country-wide metal output for household use is immense.

全國家用金屬生產量是很大量的。

🔑 Key Expression
情境表達套用語

clicks and bricks 實體和網路店面

Many traditional stores found out getting clicks and bricks strategy is a great way to both serve and keep shoppers.

許多傳統商店已經發現打實體和網路店面策略，才能同時服務和留住消費者。

Unit 17

Consequences
結果

> Deal!
> 成交！

They officially launched the building project after signing the contract.
簽了合約之後，他們正式啓動這個建案。

commitment (noun) 承諾

定義 ▸ the promise to give for something

常用搭配語 ▸ adj + commitment

lifelong		終生的承諾
personal		個人的承諾
passionate	**commitment**	熱情的承諾
firm		堅定的承諾

◈ 實用例句 ···

firm commitment 具體承諾

The government refused to give a firm commitment on labor pensions.
政府拒絕在勞工退休金上具體承諾。

efficiency (noun) 效率

定義 ▶ the condition that you can get more without wasting

常用搭配語 ▶ adj + efficiency

greater		更好的效率
productive	**efficiency**	生產的效率

verb + efficiency

achieve		達成效率
decrease	**efficiency**	降低效率

◈ 實用例句 ·····················

productive efficiency 產能
They finally maximized the productive efficiency by using this machine.
他們終於靠這台機器加大了產能。

grant (noun) 補助 / 獎學金

定義 ▶ a sum of money given by government, university or organization for a person to use on something special

常用搭配語 ▶ verb + grant

apply for		申請補助
receive		得到補助
offer	**grant**	提供補助
cut		中斷補助

◈ 實用例句 ·····················

full student grant 全額獎學金
I am so thrill that I received the full student grant this year.
拿到今年全額獎學金我超級開心的。

project (noun) 專案

定義 ▶ a piece of planned work or activity for you to achieve your particular goal

successful		成功的專案
joint	**project**	雙方合作的專案
educational		教育專案
research		研究專案

◇ 實用例句 ·······························

building project 建案
They officially launched the building project after signing the contract.
簽了合約之後，他們正式啓動這個建案。

respond (verb) 回應

定義 ▸ to react, do or say something in reply

常用搭配語 ▸ respond + adv

	accordingly	相對地回應
respond	positively	正面地回應
	immediately	立即地回應
	emotionally	激動地回應

◇ 實用例句 ·······························

responded emotionally 激動
We responded emotionally to the night view in Taipei.
看到台北夜景我們都很激動。

🔑 Key Expression
情境表達套用語

end up 最後…而是
They ended up walking home instead of taking taxi.
他們最後沒搭計程車而是走路回家。

Crime & Punishment
罪與罰

Learn a lesson from me!
不要學我。

Never ever associate with criminals.
絕對不要跟罪犯有往來。

commit (verb) 犯…罪

定義 → to do something wrong or illegal

常用搭配語 → adv + commit

	commit	
sinfully		惡意地犯罪
deliberately		故意地犯罪
fearlessly		大膽地犯罪
vulgarly		通俗地犯罪

實用例句 ·

vilely commit 卑劣的犯…罪
He vilely committed a crime in kidnapping a rich kid.
他很卑劣的綁架了一個有錢人的小孩。

criminal (noun) 罪犯

定義 ▸ a person who has committed a crime

常用搭配語 ▸ adj + criminal

habitual		慣犯
dangerous		危險罪犯
convicted	**criminal**	已被判罪的罪犯
known		眾所皆知的罪犯

實用例句

Never ever associate with criminals.
絕對不要跟罪犯有往來。

evidence (noun) 證據

定義 ▸ something that can help prove something is true or not true

常用搭配語 ▸ adj + evidence

first-hand		第一手的證據
false		假證
considerable	**evidence**	足夠的證據
crucial		關鍵證據

實用例句

false evidence 假證
She finally admitted giving the false evidence to the jury.
她最後向陪審團坦承作假證。

accuse (verb) 控告

定義 ▸ to say someone is doing something wrong or committing a crime.

常用搭配語 ▸ adv + accuse

openly		公開地控告
angrily	**accuse**	氣憤地控告
practically		幾乎要控告

實用例句 ·

openly accuse 公開地控告
I openly accused my neighbor Sally of stealing my bike.
我公開地控告我鄰居莎莉偷我腳踏車。

offend (verb) 冒犯

定義 ➤ to upset or hurt someone's feeling by being rude or lack of respect

常用搭配語 ➤ adv + offend

deeply		深深地冒犯
easily	**offend**	容易地冒犯
mortally		非常地生氣 暴怒

實用例句 ·

Each one of us should be careful not to offend people we care.
我們每個人應該要注意不要冒犯到我們在意的人。

Sorry, I really am! I didn't mean to offend you!
我真的很抱歉！我不是有意要冒犯你。

Key Expression
情境表達套用語

dismiss the case 駁回本案
The judge dismissed the case due to lack of evidence.
法官因缺乏證據駁回本案。

Unit
19

Cultures & Countries
文化與國家

I'm fond of traveling.
我喜歡旅行。

I am so keen to explore more in Europe this time.
這次我可要好好的探索歐洲。

explore (verb) 探索 / 冒險

定義 ▶ to travel around, to search

常用搭配語 ▶ adv + explore

adventurously		探索大膽地冒險
untiringly	explore	不厭倦地

verb + explore

be keen to		興致勃勃地去探索
continue to	explore	持續去探索

◈ 實用例句 ·······························

explore more 好好的探索
I am so keen to explore more in Europe this time.
這次我可要好好的探索歐洲。

individual (noun) 人 / 個體

定義 ▸ a person or thing

常用搭配語 ▸ adj + individual

average		一般人
outstanding	**individual**	非常人
autonomous		自主的人
like-minded		興趣相投 同道中人

◇ 實用例句 ‧‧

like-minded individuals 同道中人

This club is comprised of group of like-minded individuals who love travelling.
這個社團是由一群都熱愛旅行的同道中人所組成的。

culture (noun) 文化

定義 ▸ the customs, ideas, and beliefs of a group of people

常用搭配語 ▸ adj + culture

street		街頭文化
business		商業文化
local		當地文化
alien		異國文化
ancient	**culture**	古老文化
urban		都會文化
primitive		原始文化
traditional		傳統文化
dominant		佔多數的文化

◇ 實用例句 ‧‧

foster culture of 提倡……文化

If I were a president in this company, I would definitely foster culture of open communication for better efficiency.
如果我是這家公司的老闆，我一定會提倡開放溝通的文化好促進效率。

urban culture 都會文化
Taipei is the capital of Taiwan, where it is famous for urban culture.
身為首都的台北以都會文化聞名。

country (noun) 國家

定義 a nation that has its own government and people

常用搭配語 adj + country

host		主辦國家
oil-exporting		石油出口國家
overseas	country	外國
low-income		低收入國家
neighboring		鄰近國家
English-speaking		說英語的國家

實用例句

fascinating country 超棒的國家
I always tell my foreign friends that Taiwan is a fascinating country to visit!
我總是跟我的國外朋友說台灣是個值得來玩的國家。

experience (noun) 經驗

定義 the process of seeing, doing and feeling things that happen to you

常用搭配語 adj + experience

valuable		寶貴的經驗
previous		先前的經驗
work	experience	工作經驗
hands-on		從做中學的經驗

awesome experience 很讚的經驗

To be honest, I didn't get paid well but it is an awesome experience for me to work with great people there.

老實說，我薪水很低但是在那跟很棒的人工作是很讚的經驗。

hands-on experience 從中學到的經驗

I really enjoy hands-on experience of cooking in particular.

我真的熱愛從作菜中學到經驗。

Key Expression
情境表達套用語

culture shock 文化衝擊

It is common that people would experience culture shock when they travel to other countries.

當大家到外地旅遊體驗到文化衝擊是再正常不過了。

Days, Months & Seasons
日、月和季節

I hate being typical. I need something for a change.
我討厭一成不變，
我要需變化一下。

I am sick and tired of doing the same thing day after day !
我真的厭倦了一天又一天重複同樣的事！

day (noun) 天

定義 a period of 24 hours, including day light to midnight

常用搭配語 adj + day

the other		前幾天
the following / next		接下來這幾天
the previous		前天
the very / the same	day	同一天 / 當天
auspicious		好日子 / 黃道吉日
red-letter		大日子
pay		發薪日

the other day 前幾天

Hey Mel, you know I was in your area the other day. Too shame that we can't get together and grab a bite for lunch.

嗨！梅兒，你知道嗎？我前幾天剛好在你家附近，沒能跟你午餐聚一聚吃點東西真是太可惜了！

month (noun) 月

定義 ➤ a period of 4 weeks

常用搭配語 ➤ adj + month

the past few		過去這幾個月
the future		下個月
consecutive	**month**	連續這個月
alternate		每隔一個月

實用例句 ··

past few months 過去這幾個月

Things have been quite hectic for the past few months.

過去這幾個月事情有夠多。

season (noun) 季節

定義 ➤ four parts of a year, or a period when activities takes place

常用搭配語 ➤ adj + season

dry / wet		乾季 / 濕季
tourist		旅遊旺季
peak/high	**season**	旺季
off		淡季
festive season		節慶旺季

peak season 旺季
I hate going places during the peak season, it is overcrowded!
我超討厭旺季出遊，到處都是人山人海！

festival season 節慶旺季
Let's pack and hit Spain. It's festival season now.
咱們打包殺去西班牙，現在那裡是節慶的季節。

break (noun) 休息

定義 ▸ short time of rest

常用搭配語 ▸ adj + break

10-minute		十分鐘休息
lunch	**break**	午休
coffee		喝咖啡休息一下

verb + break

have a / take a		休息一下
need a	**break**	須要休息一下

◈ 實用例句 ∙∙

take a break 休息一下
Let's go out for lunch and take a coffee break. It is going to be another battle for us in the afternoon.
讓我們出去吃個午餐順便休息一下，今天下午我們可有得忙了。

need a break 需要休息一下
I'm so worn out. I really need a break from my work.
我累死了，我真的需要不工作休息一下。

schedule (noun) 行程

定義 ▶ a plan of things that need to be done

常用搭配語 ▶ adj + schedule

daily / weekly		每日 / 每周
tight		行程緊湊
business		商業行程計畫
flight / television	**schedule**	班機表 / 節目表
ambitious		充滿幹勁的行程
rigid		呆版僵硬的行程
training / work		訓練 / 工作表

◈ **實用例句** •

right on the schedule 按行程進行
Worry not, buddy. Our project is right on the schedule.
兄弟，安啦！我們的案子一切按排程進行。

Key Expression
情境表達套用語

day after day 日復一日
I am sick and tired of doing the same thing day after day！
我真的厭倦了一天又一天重複同樣的事！

Unit 21 | **Directions**

方向

Follow your nose for about 100 meters and that's it!
往前走約 100 公尺就到了。

There was a cute foreigner asking for direction on my way to lunch.
我去吃午餐的途中有一個帥氣的老外跟我問路。

follow (verb) 跟隨

定義 ▶ go after someone or something

常用搭配語 ▶ adv + follow

closely		緊緊地跟著
blindly	**follow**	盲目地跟著
dutifully		盡職地跟著

◇ 實用例句 ···

follow him 跟著他

My tour guide beckoned me to follow him.
我的導遊向我招手示意要跟著他。

followed closely 緊緊跟著
My little daughter held my hand and followed me closely in the crowd.
我小女兒在人群中握著我的手，緊緊的跟著我。

sense (noun) 感官 / 感覺

定義 ➤ the ability that enables you to feel, see, smell...etc.

常用搭配語 ➤ adj + sense

great		明智
poor	sense	能力差
sixth		第六感 / 直覺

verb + sense

have		感受到
lose	sense	無法感受到
sharpen		提高感受力

實用例句 ·······················

sense of direction 方向感
She has excellent sense of direction. I absolutely trust her!
她的方向感極佳，我絕對信任她。

great sense 敏銳的觀察
He used his great sense for the market and suceeded in his own business.
他敏鏡的觀察市場，成功的創業了。

direction (noun) 方向

定義 ➤ where to / from

常用搭配語 ➤ adj + direction

same / opposite		同方向 / 相反方向
right / wrong		正確方向 / 錯誤方向
clockwise / anti-clockwise	**direction**	順時針方向 / 逆時針方向
upward / downward		往上 / 往下

◈ **實用例句** ••

wrong direction 走錯方向

We ought to make a U turn in next intersection as we are in the wrong direction.
我們應該在下一個紅綠燈口迴轉，因為我們走錯方向了。

distance (noun) 距離

定義 ▶ the amount of space between two points or two things

常用搭配語 ▶ adj + distance

considerable		相當遠的距離
exact		實際的距離
safe	**distance**	安全距離
braking		剎車距離

◈ **實用例句** ••

braking distance 剎車距離

Be sure to allow braking distance between cars while you are driving on highway.
當行駛高速公路時，要確保車輛之間留有剎車距離。

store (noun) 商店

定義 ▶ a place where you can get daily supplies or goods

常用搭配語 ▶ adj + store

retail		零售商店
self-service		自助式商店
chain	store	連鎖商店
convenience		便利商店
electrical		電器商城

實用例句

discount store 折扣商店
I really love to visit that discount store, which saves me a lot of money and time!
我超愛逛那家折扣商店，省了我荷包和時間。

convenience store 便利商店
To my amazement, there are five convenience store in my neighorhood.
讓我感到驚奇的是，我家附近就有五家便利商店。

Key Expression
情境表達套用語

ask for direction / give direction 問路 / 指引方向
There was a cute foreigner asking for direction on my way to lunch.
我去吃午餐的途中有一個帥氣的老外跟我問路。

Disasters
災難

> What an idot I am! I shouldn't have wasted water.
> 我真的很呆，不應該浪費水。

Washing cars is definitely not an option during the drought season.
在乾旱期洗車絕對不是一項明智之舉。

rescue (noun) 搶救 / 救援

定義 ▶ to save someone or something out of dangerous situation

常用搭配語 ▶ adj + rescue

dramatic		戲劇化的搶救
attempted	rescue	企圖嘗試的救援
air-sea		海空救援
financial		財務救援

 實用例句 ･････････････････････････････････････

came to my rescue 等到救援

I was trapped in the mountain and no one came to my rescue until the next day.
It was surely a frightening experience.
我受困在山上直到隔天才等到救援，這真是令人感到害怕的經驗。

flood (noun) 水災

定義 to fill with large amount of water

常用搭配語 flood + verb

	hit / strike	水災侵襲 / 重創
flood	inundate	水災湮沒
	cause	水災造成
	subside	水災消退

實用例句

devastating flood 強大殺傷力的水災

The devastating flood hit my neighboring town and caused hundreds of people homeless.

那具有強大殺傷力的水災重創我隔壁的鄉鎮，造成數百人無家可歸。

flood subsided 水災消退

There is a lot of things to do after the flood subsided.

大水消退後，有一堆事要做。

drought (noun) 乾旱

定義 an area where it has little or no rain at all

常用搭配語 adj + drought

terrible		可怕的乾旱
severe	**drought**	嚴重的乾旱
prolonged		延長的乾旱
summer		夏季乾旱

實用例句

drought season 旱季

Washing cars is definitely not an option during the drought season.

在乾旱期洗車絕對不是一項明智之舉。

disaster (noun) 災害

定義 → terrible things or situation

常用搭配語 → adj + disaster

awful		可怕的災害
global		全球的災害
natural		自然的災害
man-made	**disaster**	人為的災害
ecological		生態的災害
economic		經濟的災難

📚 實用例句 ·······························

Strangely enough, everyone has the feeling that disaster is imminent.
說來奇怪，大家都感覺大禍要臨頭了。

economic disaster 經濟的災難
People have been blaming this taxation policy for causing the economic disaster, and fear in stock market.
大家都責怪稅賦政策，導致經濟災難和股市恐慌。

earthquake (noun) 地震

定義 → a sudden, violent shaking of a part of the earth's surface that usually causes great damage

常用搭配語 → adj + earthquake

great		大地震
severe	**earthquake**	嚴重的地震
minor		輕微的地震

earthquake + verb

earthquake	happen	地震發生
	shake something	地震動搖
	devastate something	地震摧毀
	measuring 5.3	地震震度 5.3
	leaves people homeless	地震讓人無家可歸

實用例句

huge earthquake 巨震
The huge earthquake struck Indonesia and devastated the business center.
巨震重創印尼並摧毀了商業重鎮。

Key Expression
情境表達套用語

the shelter be occupied with 收容所充滿
The shelter is occupied with homeless victims from the earthquake.
收容所充滿了地震後無家可歸的難民。

Driving & Transportation
開車和交通工具

Saving money comes first.
省錢第一。

It saves me a lot by sharing a cab with my co-worker.
跟我同事共乘一部計程車省了我不少錢。

driver (noun) 駕駛

| 定義 | person who is driving |

| 常用搭配語 | adj + driver |

careful		小心的駕駛
reckless		粗心的駕駛
drunken		酒醉的駕駛
hit-and-run	driver	肇事逃逸的駕駛
experienced		有經驗的駕駛
inexperienced		菜鳥駕駛

實用例句 ·

reckless driver 粗心的駕駛

You are such a reckless driver! Look at the dent in my car!
妳真是個粗心的駕駛，看看我車子的凹痕！

drunken driver 酒醉的駕駛
What a bummer! My car was hit from the rear by a drunken driver.
真夠倒楣！我的車子被一個酒醉的駕駛從後面追撞。

commute (verb) 通勤

定義 to travel between where you live and where you work

常用搭配語 commute + adv

	daily / everyday	每天通勤
commute	regularly	頻繁地通勤
	continuously	持續地通勤
	efficiently	有效地通勤

實用例句

commute daily 每天通勤
I commute daily from NeiHu to Taipei by MRT.
我每天上下班靠捷運來往內湖和台北。

arrive (verb) 抵達

定義 to get to a place

常用搭配語 arrive + adv

	early / late	早 / 晚抵達
arrive	shortly / soon	很快地抵達
	on time	準時抵達
	finally	終於抵達

arrive	safe and sound	安全抵達
	unannounced	未告知的抵達

arrive in US 抵達美國
We are due to arrive in US at noon.
我們預定中午應會抵達美國。

transport (noun) 交通運輸

定義 ➤ to move things or people from one place to another

常用搭配語 ➤ adj + transport

efficient		有效的運輸
public	transport	大眾運輸
freight		貨物運輸

◈ 實用例句 ･････････････････････････････････

mass rapid transport 大眾快捷運輸
There are more and more people relying on mass rapid transport to get around in big city.
有愈來愈多的人仰賴捷運好利於在大城市中遊走。

public transportation 大眾運輸工具
One of the advantages of living in city is able to make use of public transportation.
生活在城市的好處之一，是可以善用大眾運輸工具。

visibility (noun) 能見度

定義 ➤ the ability to see how far it is

常用搭配語 ➤ adj + visibility

excellent		極佳的能見度
clear		清晰的能見度
bad	visibility	不好的能見度
limited		有限的能見度
poor		糟糕的能見度
zero		能見度零

實用例句

visibility is poor 能見度糟糕

I need to drive carefully as the visibility is poor due to the heavy rain on highway.
我可要小心開車因為高速公路大雨，能見度極差。

clear visibility 視線良好

It is a pleasue to drive around the countryside with clear visibility and fresh air.
能在視線良好和空氣新鮮的鄉野間開車，真是一大樂事。

Key Expression
情境表達套用語

share a cab 共乘一部計程車

It saves me a lot by sharing a cab with my co-worker.
跟我同事共乘一部計程車省了我不少錢。

Unit 24 | Education
教育

> I can't wait for the class break.
> 我真等不及要下課了。

That's hard-core. My college holds classes on holidays.
好硬喔（不輕鬆），我的大學連假日都照開課！

class (noun) 班級 / 課程

| 定義 | a group of students |

| 常用搭配語 | adj + class |

elementary		小學班
intermediate	**class**	中級班
advanced		進階班
evening		夜間課程

verb + class

take		上課
hold	**class**	開課
sit in on		試聽課程

🔖 實用例句 ··

hold classes 開課

That's hard-core. My college holds classes on holidays.

好硬喔（不輕鬆），我的大學連假日都照開課！

attend (verb) 參加

定義 ▶ to be at an event or go to a place

常用搭配語 ▶ adv + attend

diligently		認真地參加
regularly	attend	時常地參加
punctually		準時地參加

verb + attend

be able to		能夠參加
be unable to	attend	無法參加
be invited to		獲邀參加

🔖 實用例句 ··

be unable to attend 無法參加

It's a shame I am unable to attend the annual seminar in Tokyo this year.

我今年無法參加東京一年一度的研習會實在太可惜了。

study (noun) 學習 / 研究

定義 ▶ learning or research

常用搭配語 ▶ adj + study

full-time		全職研究
independent		獨立研究
language	study	語言學習研究
further		更進一步研究
close		深入研究
detailed case		完整案例研究

· ·

The study has shown that girls outperform boys now in school at every level.
研究顯示，學校女孩在任何程度上都超前男孩的表現。

diploma (noun) 學歷

定義 a piece of paper given by school to show that you have successfully completed a course of study

常用搭配語 adj + diploma

college		大學學歷
graduate	**diploma**	研究所學歷
national		國內學歷

verb + diploma

have/hold		擁有學歷
obtain/get	**diploma**	得到學歷
award		獲頒學歷

實用例句 ·

diploma holder 有學歷的人
It is not 100% guarantee of decent job now for diploma holders in higher education.
現在連高等學歷的人，都不能保證可以找到好工作了。

education (noun) 教育

定義 a process of learning or teaching in school

常用搭配語 adj + education

further		進修
decent		良好教育
compulsory	**education**	義務教育
vocational		技職教育

verb + education

receive		受教育
extend	**education**	加強擴展教育
complete		完成教育

實用例句

extend education 深造
I went to California to extend my education in language.
我去了加州深造我的語言教育。

compulsory education 義務教育
Compulsory education in Taiwan reguired all children to attend school for certain 12 years.
台灣的義務教育規定所有孩童必須上 12 年的學校教育。

Key Expression
情境表達套用語

take training courses / classes 上訓練課程 / 上課
I am excited about taking the training course next week.
我對下星期要上的訓練課程感到很興奮。

Unit 25

Everyday activities & Advice
日常活動和小建言

> I just don't want to get up!
> 我爬不起來！

It is just so hard to break my day-to -day routine.
要打破日常慣例對我來說太難了。

joke (noun) 笑話

定義 something you said in order to make people laugh

常用搭配語 verb + joke

get		聽懂笑話
make	joke	說笑話
take		接受笑話
treat something as		把⋯⋯當笑話

◈ 實用例句 ·······························

can't take the joke 開不得玩笑
The problem is she can't take the joke, she is easily offended.
問題是她開不得玩笑，她超會生氣的。

advice (noun) 忠告

| 定義 | an idea that someone told you what you should do or act in a situation |

| 常用搭配語 | adj + advice |

sound		良好的忠告
constructive		有建設性的忠告
financial		財務忠告
medical	**advice**	醫學忠告
practical		實際忠告
impartial		客觀公正的忠告
wrong		錯誤建議

實用例句

my advice 我的忠告

My advice to you would be to get ready and give it a try again.
我對你的忠告就是準備好再試一次。

manner (noun) 方式 / 樣子

| 定義 | the way you do things |

| 常用搭配語 | adj + manner |

friendly		友善的方式
laughable		可笑的方式
odd	**manner**	怪異的方式
impatient		不耐煩的樣子

實用例句

friendly manner 友善的方式

I really like that, she always speaks in a friendly manner.
我真喜歡她總是友善說話的樣子。

professional manner 專業的方式

This problem needs to be handled in a more professional manner.

這問題需要用專業的方式來處理。

routine (noun) 慣例 / 常規 / 例行公事

定義　　a usual way of doing things

常用搭配語　　adj + routine

day-to-day		日常慣例
office	**routine**	工作慣例

verb + routine

get into		養成慣例
follow	**routine**	遵守常規
break		打破常規

實用例句 ·······················

day-to-day routine 日常慣例

It is just so hard to break my day-to -day routine.

要打破日常慣例對我來說太難了。

clean (adj) 乾淨

定義　　pure or free of dirt

常用搭配語　　adv + clean

pretty		非常乾淨
almost	**clean**	幾乎很乾淨
spotlessly		一塵不染

verb + clean

look		看起來乾淨
wipe something	**clean**	抹乾淨
keep		保持乾淨

💠 實用例句 ·····························

clean and tidy 乾淨整齊
I always keep my bedroom clean and tidy.
我總是讓我的臥室保持乾淨又整齊。

I think I'll just wear whtatever it's clean for the date.
我想我就穿只要是乾淨的衣服赴約就好了。

clean freak 潔癖
I can tell that Adale is a clean freak . She always keeps her cubicle spotlessly
clean.
不難知道艾黛兒是個有潔癖的人，她的工作空間總是一塵不染。

Key Expression
情境表達套用語

ran into an issue with something 惹上麻煩
My father ran into an issue with some rental property stuff. He might need my
hand.
我老爸惹上了一些房地產上的麻煩，他可能需要我幫忙。

Failure
失敗

It's all my fault .
Please forgive me.
都是我的錯，請原諒我。

I raised my hand in mock surrender after three-week cold war with my wife.
在跟我老婆冷戰 3 星期後，我把雙手舉起假裝投降。

confess (verb) 坦承

定義 ▸ to admit that you have done something wrong or your unwillingness that something is true

常用搭配語 ▸ adv + confess

openly		公開地坦承
ruefully		後悔地坦承
tearfully	**confess**	哭著坦承
belatedly		事後坦承
blushingly		臉紅地坦承

◇ 實用例句 ··

get something to confess 招認某事

I have got something to confess-I looked through your phone.
我要承認一件事——我有偷看過你的手機。

failure (noun) 失敗

定義 ▶ something you learned when you didn't get what you want

Not successful

常用搭配語 ▶ adj + failure

personal		個人失敗
economic	**failure**	經濟上的失敗
inevitable		不可避免的失敗
complete		完全的失敗

verb + failure

avoid		避免失敗
admit	**failure**	承認失敗
be doomed to		註定要失敗

◈ 實用例句 ‧‧‧

admit the failure 承認失敗

The professor is too proud to admit the failure in his management.

那個教授太驕傲到無法承認自己管理上的失敗。

surrender (noun) 投降

定義 ▶ stop fighting and admit defeat

常用搭配語 ▶ adj + surrender

forced		被逼的投降
unconditional	**surrender**	無條件的投降
instant		立刻投降

◈ 實用例句 ‧‧‧

in mock surrender 假裝投降

I raised my hand in mock surrender after three-week cold war with my wife.

在跟我老婆冷戰 3 星期後，我把雙手舉起假裝投降。

reform (noun) 改革 / 改進

定義 to become better

常用搭配語 adj + reform

radical		根本的改革
educational	**reform**	教育的改革
welfare		福利的改革
administrative		行政的改革

實用例句

social reform 社會改革

People will march on the street to call for a social reform.
大眾將會走上街頭要求社會改革。

risk (noun) 風險 / 危險

定義 danger

常用搭配語 verb + risk

run		承擔風險
incur	**risk**	遭受危險
minimize		將風險降到最低
assess		評估風險

實用例句

I can't afford to run such a high risk!
我無法承擔如此高的風險。

Key Expression
情境表達套用語

going nowhere 沒進展 / 沒出息 (人)
I feel so upset that my research is going nowhere.
我那無法突破的研究讓我很沮喪。

Unit 27

Family & Friends
家庭和朋友

> I'm the happiest adopted kid ever.
> 我是最快樂的被領養小孩。

The social workers help abused kids find a decent adoptive family.
社工人員幫助被虐孩童找到一個相當不錯的領養家庭。

family (noun) 家庭

定義 a social group of parents, children and others who are related

常用搭配語 adj + family

well-to-do		富裕的家庭
low-income		低收入的家庭
single-parent	**family**	單親的家庭
adoptive		領養的家庭
middle-class		中產階級的家庭

實用例句 ·····················

adoptive family 領養的家庭
The social workers help abused kids find a decent adoptive family.
社工人員幫助被虐孩童找到一個相當不錯的領養家庭。

relation (noun) 關係

定義 ▸ connection between two things / people

常用搭配語 ▸ adj + relation

direct		直系親屬
close	**relation**	密切的關係
harmonious		和諧的關係

📚 實用例句 ··

have no relation with 跟 …… 一點關係都沒有

I have no relation with Amy, but we look so much alike!

我跟 Amy 不是直系親屬，我們兩個長得很像耶！

relatives (noun) 親戚

定義 ▸ a member of your family

常用搭配語 ▸ adj + relatives

close		近親
distant	**relatives**	遠親
elderly		年長的親戚

📚 實用例句 ··

Gary is my relative by marriage. My brother married his sister.

Gary 是我的姻親，他姊姊嫁給了我哥哥。

friend (noun) 朋友

定義 ▸ a person you like a lot and know well

常用搭配語 ▸ adj + friend

intimate		親密的朋友
lifelong	**friend**	一生的朋友
female		女性的朋友

fair-weather		酒肉朋友
mutual	**friend**	共同的朋友

📚 實用例句 ••

mutual friend 共同的朋友
I know John through our mutual friend Max.
我透過我們共同的朋友 Max 認識 John 的。

friendship (noun) 友誼

定義 ▶ the state of being friends

常用搭配語 ▶ adj + friendship

deep		深厚的友誼
everlasting	**friendship**	長久的友誼

📚 實用例句 ••

token of friendship 友誼的信物
I gave Colin a pot of plant as a token of our friendship. And he loves it !
我給 Colin 一盆植物當作友誼的信物,他愛不釋手!

🔑 Key Expression
情境表達套用語

next of kin 直系親屬
Only will the next of kin be informed the air crash.
只有直系親屬會被通知有關空難的消息。

Unit 28 | **Films & Other Media**
電影和其他媒體

Life was like a box of chocolates. you never know of what you're gonna get.
生命就像一盒巧克力，
你永遠也不知道將拿到什麼。

The movie I saw last night was fabulous and inspired me a lot.
我昨晚看的電影超正點又啟發我心。

actor / actress (noun) 男 / 女演員

定義 ▶ a person who plays a character in a movie or a play

常用搭配語 ▶ adj + actor / actress

born		天生的男 / 女演員
talented		有才華的男 / 女演員
veteran	actor / actress	資深的男 / 女演員
sought-after		走紅的男 / 女演員
unemployed		沒人要的男 / 女演員
supporting		配角男 / 女演員

◇ 實用例句 ••••••••••••••••••••••••••••••••

My uncle is a born actor; he enjoys performing on the stage for audience.
我叔叔是個天生的演員，他熱愛為觀眾在舞台上演出。

host / hostess (noun) 男 / 女主持人

定義 a person who entertain visitors or appear on TV program or radio

常用搭配語 adj + host / hostess

talk-show		談話節目男 / 女主持人
generous	**host / hostess**	大方的男 / 女主持人
plump		豐滿的男 / 女主持人
cheerful		開心的男 / 女主持人

實用例句

plump hostess 豐滿的女主持人

I enjoy watching a talk show by a plump hostess; she is bright and always maintaining the cheerful outlook.

我喜歡看豐滿的女主持人主持的那個談話節目；她聰明又笑口常開。

director (noun) 導演

定義 a person who organizes a film or a play

常用搭配語 adj + director

potential		有潛力的導演
prominent		有名的導演
independent	**director**	獨立導演
executive		首席導演
assistant		助理導演

實用例句

We are all keen to see the movie made by prominent director Ang Lee.

我們大家都好期待台灣之光李安導演的電影。

acting (noun) 演技

定義 to perform the role of a character in a play or a movie

常用搭配語 adj + acting

brilliant		絕佳的演技
wooden	**acting**	呆板的演技
unconvincing		沒說服力的演技

實用例句 ·····································

unconvincing acting 超爛演技

His unconvincing acting spoiled the whole movie.

他的超爛演技成為那部電影的最大敗筆。

movie (noun) 電影

定義 a recording of moving images about telling a story for people to watch it in theater or on TV

常用搭配語 adj + movie

great		很棒的電影
smash-hit		賣座的電影
cult	**movie**	異風格電影
low-budget		低成本電影
In-flight		飛機上播放的電影

實用例句 ·····································

The movie I saw last night was fabulous and inspired me a lot.

我昨晚看的電影超正點又啟發我心。

Key Expression
情境表達套用語

tune in the radio 收聽廣播

Be sure to tune in to the movie reviews on the radio!

務必要收聽廣播上的電影回顧喔！

Flying
飛航

> There is nothing to fear...
> 沒什麼好怕的。

My outbound flight to Boston was smooth, however, the return flight was so bumpy.
我去 Boston 的飛行順暢，但我的回程飛行很不穩。

flight (noun) 飛行

定義 journey on the plane

常用搭配語 adj + flight

outbound		去程飛行
return		回程飛行
scheduled		預計飛行
direct	**flight**	直飛
long-distance		長途飛行
bumpy		飛行不穩

實用例句 ·····················

My outbound flight to Boston was smooth, however, the return flight was so bumpy.
我去 Boston 的飛行順暢，但我的回程飛行很不穩。

departure (noun) 離境前往

定義 leaving for a place

常用搭配語 adj + departure

sudden		匆忙離境前往
hasty	departure	快速離境前往
flight		班機離境前往

實用例句 ···

Wendy made a hasty departure to visit her sick mom in Japan.
Wendy 快速離境前往日本探視她生病的媽媽。

arrival (noun) 抵達

定義 acting of getting to a place

常用搭配語 adj + arrival

early		提早抵達
delayed	arrival	延後抵達
timely		準時抵達
unexpected		未預期的抵達

實用例句 ···

upon my arrival 我一抵達
My family picked me up sooner upon my arrival.
我的家人在我一抵達就來接我了。

welcome (verb) 歡迎

定義 to be happy to see someone

常用搭配語 adv + welcome

heartily	welcome	真心地歡迎
formally		正式地歡迎

⬡ 實用例句 ••

They are looking forward to welcoming the new manager to the company.
他們正期待歡迎公司的新經理。

luggage (noun) 行李

定義 → the bags or containers that you take with you when travelling

常用搭配語 → verb + luggage

carry		攜帶行李
check in		登記行李
claim	luggage	提領行李
pack		打包行李
unload		取出行李

⬡ 實用例句 ••

unload the luggage 取出行李
The bus driver helped us unload the luggage of our tour group.
巴士司機幫我們拿出旅行團的行李。

Key Expression
情境表達套用語

go through the custom 通過海關
He was stopped by the custom inspector when he went through the custom.
當他在過海關時，他被海關檢查員攔了下來。

Unit 30

Food, Drinks & Groceries
食物、飲料和雜貨

> Sugar promotes excessive food intake in obese people.
> 糖會引發肥胖族攝取過多食物。

The doctor told me that I have excessively consumed sugar.
醫生告訴我攝取過多的糖分。

ingredient (noun) 原料

定義 something that is used to make food

常用搭配語 adj + ingredient

raw		生原料
dry		乾原料
natural		天然原料
artificial	**ingredient**	人工原料
exotic		外國原料
secret		秘密原料
major		主要原料

實用例句 ·

major ingredient 主要原料

The major ingredients for cookies are butter and sugar.
這餅乾的主要原料是奶油和糖。

appetite (noun) 胃口

定義 desire for food

常用搭配語 verb + appetite

have		有胃口
lose		沒胃口
regain		重新得到胃口
give someone	appetite	讓人有胃口
increase		增加胃口
curb / suppress		抑制胃口
spoil		壞了胃口

實用例句

spoiled my appetite 壞了胃口
That chunk of cheese cake spoiled my appetite before dinner.
那一塊起士蛋糕壞了我吃晚餐的胃口。

eater (noun) 飲食者

定義 a person who is eating food

常用搭配語 adj + eater

meat		肉食者
picky	eater	挑食者
light		吃很少的人
healthy		吃的健康的人

實用例句

light eater 吃很少的人
Don't be such a light eater! Eat some more of what I made for you specially.
別吃的那麼少嘛，再多吃一點我特別為你做的菜。

consume (verb) 吃喝

定義 ➤ to eat or drink something

常用搭配語 ➤ adv + consume

insufficiently		不夠地吃喝
excessively	**consume**	過多地吃喝
noisily		吵鬧地吃喝

◈ 實用例句 ·····································

excessively consume 攝取過多

The doctor told me that I have excessively consumed sugar.
醫生告訴我攝取過多的糖分。

book / reserve (verb) 預訂 / 保留

定義 ➤ to keep something for your use

常用搭配語 ➤ adv + book / reserve

specially		特別預訂保留
exclusively	**book / reserve**	專門預訂保留
fully		全數預訂保留

◈ 實用例句 ·····································

This parking space is normally reserved for dinning customers in our restaurant.
這個停車位通常是保留給來我們餐廳用晚餐的客戶。

Key Expression
情境表達套用語

grab a bite 隨便吃個東西
Let's grab a bite before the meeting.
我看我們開會前隨便吃個東西吧！

Friends & Colleagues
朋友和同事

We see a lot of thing in common on painting.
我們兩個人對繪畫
都看法一致。

Jane and I share the common interest, that's why we spend a lot of time together.
我和 Jane 有共同的興趣，這也是我們常在一起的原因。

harmony (noun) 和諧

定義 ▶ a happy situation without disagreement for the two

常用搭配語 ▶ adj + harmony

perfect		完美的和諧
domestic		家庭的和諧
social	harmony	社會的和諧
political		政治的和諧
racial		種族的和諧

◈ 實用例句 ∙∙∙∙∙∙∙∙∙∙∙∙∙∙∙∙∙∙∙∙∙∙∙∙∙∙∙∙∙∙∙∙∙∙∙∙∙∙∙

great harmony 相處和睦
I often envy my parents living together in great harmony.
我常常羨慕我父母親相處和睦。

atmosphere (noun) 氣氛

定義 ▸ a general feeling of an environment

常用搭配語 ▸ adj + atmosphere

friendly		友善的氣氛
cozy		舒適的氣氛
romantic	**atmosphere**	浪漫的氣氛
hostile		敵對的氣氛
carnival		歡樂的氣氛

◈ 實用例句 •••••••••••••••••••••••••••••••••••••••

His loudness and rudeness really ruined the atmosphere.
他的孤僻和沒禮貌壞了氣氛。

interest (noun) 興趣

定義 ▸ you want to be involved with and learn or hear more of something

常用搭配語 ▸ adj + interest

strong		強烈的興趣
considerable		相當多的興趣
widespread		廣泛的興趣
growing	**interest**	逐漸喜歡的興趣
personal		個人的興趣
media		媒體的興趣

◈ 實用例句 •••••••••••••••••••••••••••••••••••••••

Jane and I share the common interest, that's why we spend a lot of time together.
我和 Jane 有共同的興趣，這也是我們常在一起的原因。

associate (noun) 同事夥伴

定義 ▸ a friend or partner you work with or spend time with

常用搭配語 ▸ adj + associate

former		之前的同事
close	associate	密友
business		生意夥伴
political		政治夥伴

實用例句

He has made up his mind. Neither his friends nor associates could change his mind.
他已下定決心了，他的朋友或同事都無法動搖他的決定。

help (noun) 幫助

定義 to give someone a hand to make things easier or deal with a problem

常用搭配語 adj + help

real		真正的幫助
direct		直接的幫助
mutual		相互的幫助
voluntary	help	義務的幫助
outside		外來的幫助
immediate		立即的幫助
medical		醫療的幫助

實用例句

mutual-help 相互的幫助
Let us hope to build up a mutual-help society and make it a better place!
讓我們期望建立相互的幫助來幫助社會變得更好。

Key Expression
情境表達套用語

sour friendship 讓友誼變質
Money issue will sour your friendship.
金錢問題會讓友誼變質。

Getting around
到處逛逛

Be sure to wear sun glasses
and apply sun block.
一定要帶太陽眼鏡、
擦防曬油。

Let us get sunbath on the beach for a change.
讓我們去海邊作日光浴換換口味。

journey (noun) 旅程

定義 ▶ a trip

常用搭配語 ▶ adj + journey

homeward		回家的旅程
arduous		艱困的旅程
tiring	journey	疲累的旅程
two-month		二個月的旅程
wasted		白跑一趟

🍃 實用例句 ·····························

He wasn't in town, which means we made a wasted journey. Daaaaaah....
他根本就出遠門了，也就是說我們白跑一趟了，笨喔……

traveler (noun) 旅者

> 定義 ━━ a person who goes on a trip / journey

> 常用搭配語 ━━ adj + traveler

tired		疲累的旅者
seasoned	**traveler**	有經驗的旅者
frequent		常旅行的人
business		出公差的人

◇ 實用例句 ‧‧‧‧‧‧‧‧‧‧‧‧‧‧‧‧‧‧‧‧‧‧‧‧‧‧

unwary travelers 不設防的旅者

Egypt has been a notorious country for unwary travelers.

埃及對一些不設防的旅者而言是個惡名昭彰的國家。

landscape (noun) 景觀

> 定義 ━━ a view of a large area

> 常用搭配語 ━━ adj + landscape

urban		都市景觀
bleak	**landscape**	荒涼的景觀
rural		鄉村景觀
breathtaking		令人屏息的景觀

◇ 實用例句 ‧‧‧‧‧‧‧‧‧‧‧‧‧‧‧‧‧‧‧‧‧‧‧‧‧‧

Whenever I am in depression, I will visit 101 to enjoy the beautiful landscape of skyscrapers and various buildings.

每當我不開心的時候，我就會去 101 欣賞漂亮的高樓和各種建築景觀。

vehicle (noun) 車輛

> 定義 ━━ a machine for transporting people or things

> 常用搭配語 ━━ adj + vehicle

oncoming		來向的車輛
passing	vehicle	經過的車輛
parked		停放的車輛
stolen		被偷的車輛

📚 實用例句 ···

One day I saw mayor sitting in a passing vehicle when I parked my bike downstairs.
我有天在樓下停腳踏車時，看到市長的車經過。

location (noun) 位置

定義 a particular place or position

常用搭配語 adj + location

ideal		理想的位置
exact	location	精確的位置
secret		秘密的位置
convenient		位置便利

📚 實用例句 ···

on location 實地外景
This documentary was filmed on location in California.
這部紀錄片是在加州實地外景拍攝。

🔑 Key Expression
情境表達套用語

for a change 換個方式
Let us get sunbath on the beach for a change.
讓我們去海邊作日光浴換換口味。

Gestures
姿勢

I have no idea where your key is.
我沒看到你的鑰匙。

I shrugged my shoulders when my mom asked me where the car key is.
當我媽問我車鑰匙放哪時，我聳了聳肩。

gesture (noun) 手勢 / 姿勢

定義 ▸ a movement of your body that shows your idea and feeling

常用搭配語 ▸ adj + gesture

dramatic		誇張的手勢
careless	gesture	不在乎的姿勢
rude		粗魯的手勢
threatening		威脅的手勢

◇ **實用例句** ·····································

Now many teenagers make rude gestures that they learned from movies.
現在很多年輕人都會比出電影上學到的粗魯的手勢。

point (verb) 指著

定義 ➤ to get someone's attention by showing the direction with finger

常用搭配語 ➤ point + prep

point	at / in the direction of	指著……方向
	to	指向
	with	用……指著

◈ 實用例句 •

point out 指出

She rightly points out the difficulties that we are facing now.

她立刻指出了我們現正面臨的困難點。

sniff (verb) 深吸輕蔑的聲音

定義 ➤ smell, take in air through your nose

常用搭配語 ➤ verb +sniff

give / let out	**sniff**	發出不屑的聲音
take		深吸一口氣

◈ 實用例句 •

loud sniff 輕蔑的聲音

She gave a loud sniff of disapproval during my briefing.

她發出輕蔑的聲音否決我的簡介。

hand (noun) 手

定義 ➤ part of your body

常用搭配語 ➤ verb + hand

shake	**hand**	握手
wave		招手
cup		手成杯狀的動作
withdraw		手抽回

cupped my hand on the mouthpiece of my cell phone 用手摀住手機聽筒
I cupped my hand on the mouthpiece of my cell phone so my boss didn't know that I was outside the office.
我用手摀住手機聽筒,這樣我老闆才不知道我在外面鬼混。

feet (noun) 腳

| 定義 | a part of your body for moving around |

| 常用搭配語 | adj + feet |

faltering		蹣跚的腳
bare	**feet**	光腳
swollen		腫脹的腳
blistered		起水泡的腳

實用例句

We walked on the sandy beach with our bare feet. It was so relaxing!
我們光著腳在沙灘上漫步,真是令人放鬆啊!

Key Expression
情境表達套用語

shrug shoulders 聳肩
I shrugged my shoulders when my mom asked me where the car key is.
當我媽問我車鑰匙放哪時,我聳了聳肩。

Health & Sickness

健康與疾病

Three times a day;
take one after each meal.
1 日三次，飯後服用 1 顆。

Pharmacy

Take this pill. This is what I take when I need to kill my pain.
把這藥丸吃下去，這是我需要止痛時吃的藥。

infection (noun) 感染

定義	a disease caused by germs

常用搭配語	adj + infection

acute		急性感染
minor		輕微感染
chronic	infection	長期感染
recurrent		復發感染
respiratory		呼吸感染

◈ 實用例句 ••••••••••••••••••••••••••••••••••

As we know that people with lower immunity are prone to the infection.
就如同我們所知的免疫力低下的人容易感染生病。

injury (noun) 傷害

定義 ▸ got hurt: caused someone to not be in healthy condition

常用搭配語 ▸ adj + injury

appalling		可怕的傷害
permanent	**injury**	永久的傷害
accidental		意外的傷害
internal		內在的傷害

◈ 實用例句 ·····································

internal injury in organs 內部器官傷害
That severe car accident could cause internal injury in organs.
那個嚴重車禍可能導致內部器官傷害。

temperature (noun) 溫度

定義 ▸ the measured amount of heat or coolness in an area or in the body

常用搭配語 ▸ adj + temperature

extreme		極端溫度
surface		表面溫度
boiling		沸點
daytime	**temperature**	日間溫度
global		全球溫度
average		平均溫度

◈ 實用例句 ·····································

Yesterday my hometown reached its highest temperature for the past few weeks.
昨天我住的地方溫度達到過去這幾個星期的最高溫了。

pain (noun) 痛

定義 ▸ a very bad feeling from illness or injury that you want to stop it

常用搭配語 ▸ adj + pain

burning		灼熱的痛
excruciating	**pain**	劇烈的痛
sudden		突然的痛
intermittent		間歇性的痛

◇ **實用例句** ●

kill my pain 止痛

Take this pill. This is what I take when I need to kill my pain.

把這藥丸吃下去，這是我需要止痛時吃的藥。

fever (noun) 發燒

定義 high temperature in your body when you are sick

常用搭配語 verb + fever

come down with		因發燒病倒
run	**fever**	發高燒
reduce		退燒
be accompanied by		伴隨高燒

◇ **實用例句** ●

reduce high fever 退高燒

I got some pills from the doctor to reduce my high fever.

我從醫生那邊拿藥好退高燒。

Key Expression
情境表達套用語

take medicine / pill 吃藥 / 服藥

Take this pill twice a day with lots of water, I am sure you will get better the next day. 這藥丸配大量開水一天二次，我相信隔天你就會好多了。

Unit 35 | **Holidays**
假日

> My muscles relaxed.
> 我的肌肉放鬆了。

Take a deep breath and try to relax little by little.
深呼吸,試著慢慢地放鬆。

hotel (noun) 旅館

> **定義** ▶ a place where you need to pay for a room to stay or sleep

> **常用搭配語** ▶ adj + hotel

family-run		家庭經營的旅館
nearby		附近的旅館
seafront	hotel	面海的旅館
luxury		豪華的旅館
five-star		五星級的旅館

verb + hotel

book		預訂旅館
check in	hotel	入住旅館
check out		退房

running this hotel 經營這家旅館
My family has been running this hotel for the past 20 years.
我的家族經營這家旅館已 20 年。

holiday (noun) 假期

定義 ▬ the day you can stay away from work or school

常用搭配語 ▬ verb + holiday

go on / have / take		去渡假
book	**holiday**	預訂假期
cancel		取消假期

◇ 實用例句 ···························

My boss isn't in right now, he has gone on oversea holidays with his family.
我老闆現在不在，他跟他的家人去國外度假了。

getaway (noun) 放鬆之旅程 / 地

定義 ▬ a place where you go for a relaxation

常用搭配語 ▬ adj + getaway

weekend		周末放鬆之旅
small		精緻之旅
dreamy	**getaway**	夢幻之旅
peaceful		寧靜之旅

◇ 實用例句 ···························

2-week sweet getaway 2 星期的甜蜜之旅
I have been swamped with my work for the past few months. I desperately need a
2-week sweet getaway.
過去幾個月我已經忙到爆，我超級需要啟動我的二週甜蜜之旅。

weekend getaway 週末放鬆之旅

With the fad of two-day weekend, everyone now can enjoy a weekend getaway.

隨著週休二日的風潮，大家都能享受週末放鬆之旅。

relax (verb) 放鬆

定義 to make yourself become calm and comfortable

常用搭配語 adv + relax

deeply		深度地放鬆
simply		簡單地放鬆
visibly		看的見地放鬆
completely	**relax**	完全地放鬆
gradually		逐漸地放鬆
slowly		緩慢地放鬆

◈ 實用例句 ·····································

relax little by little 慢慢地放鬆

Take a deep breath and try to relax little by little.

深呼吸，試著慢慢地放鬆。

simply relax 簡單地放鬆

All you have to do is simply relax and follow the yoga teacher.

你所要做的就是簡單地放鬆和跟著瑜伽老師的動作。

city (noun) 城市

定義 an area where many people live and a lot of business go on

常用搭配語 adj + city

livable		可居住的城市
capital		首都
coastal	**city**	海岸城市
twin		友好城市

My family and I live in the outskirt of the city as we can't afford the high rent in the city.
我和我的家人住在城市郊區，因為市區的房價我們可租不起。

coastal city 海洋城市
I wish I could afford to live in a coastal city where I can wake up by the sound of the ocean.
我真希望住得起海洋城市，可以讓我聽海洋的聲音起床。

Key Expression
情境表達套用語

take time off 休假
I really need to take some time off after this arduous work.
在這個艱難的工作後，我真的需要休假一下。

Houses & Housing
房屋與住宅

> May I borrow some salt from you?
> 可以借我一些鹽巴嗎？

Sally has been a very friendly neighbor to me.
Sally 對我來說一直是個非常友善的好鄰居。

neighbor (noun) 鄰居

> 定義 ▸ person who live next to your door

> 常用搭配語 ▸ adj + neighbor

eccentric		古怪的鄰居
irrational	**neighbor**	不理性的鄰居
next-door		隔壁的鄰居

◇ 實用例句 ···

Sally has been a very friendly neighbor to me.
Sally 對我來說一直是個非常友善的好鄰居。

neighborhood (noun) 附近地區

> 定義 ▸ the area around your house

常用搭配語	adj + neighborhood	
poor		貧窮的附近地區
residential	**neighborhood**	居住的附近地區
whole		整個附近地區

◈ 實用例句 ·····································

around my neighborhood 我家附近
There are 2 lush parks around my neighborhood.
我家附近有兩個綠油油的公園。

furniture (noun) 家具

定義	bed, chair and table that are used to make a house ready for use

常用搭配語	adj + furniture	
antique		骨董家具
cheap	**furniture**	便宜家具
second-hand		二手家具
rattan		藤製家具

◈ 實用例句 ·····································

completed with furniture 家具俱全
I need to rent an apartment completed with furniture for my future job.
我為了未來的工作需要租一間家具俱全的公寓。

tenant (noun) 房客

定義	person who rents or leases a house from a landlord

常用搭配語	adj + tenant	
former		前任房客
sitting	**tenant**	現任房客
potential		未來房客

實用例句 ‥‥‥‥‥‥‥‥‥‥‥‥‥‥‥‥‥‥‥‥‥‥‥‥‥‥‥

student tenant 學生房客

This property is now occupied by 2 student tenants and there is one more room available for the last tenant.

這棟房子現在住著二個學生房客，還有一間空房留給最後一位房客。

community (noun) 社區

| 定義 | a group of people lived in the same area |

| 常用搭配語 | adj + community |

thriving		繁榮的社區
immigrant	**community**	移民的社區
local		當地的社區

實用例句 ‥‥‥‥‥‥‥‥‥‥‥‥‥‥‥‥‥‥‥‥‥‥‥‥‥‥‥

whole community 全社區

The pollution problem has raised the concerns for the whole community.

汙染的問題已經引起全社區的關注。

Key Expression
情境表達套用語

residential area 住宅區

The residential area I live is close to school district.

我居住的社區離學區很近。

Housework
家事

Rug my floor to beautify my place.
擺放地毯，可美化環境。

I am thinking about putting a rug on my living floor.
我在想要在我的客廳地板鋪地毯。

floor (noun) 地板

定義 the part of a room on which you stand

常用搭配語 adj + floor

carpeted		有地毯的地板
polished	**floor**	磨亮的地板
tiled		磁磚地板
wooden		木質地板

實用例句

living floor 客廳地板

I am thinking about putting a rug on my living floor.
我在想要在我的客廳地板鋪地毯。

chore (noun) 瑣事

定義 ► a tiny thing that needs to be done as a routine

常用搭配語 ► adj + chore

weary		煩人的瑣事
daily	**chore**	日常瑣事
household		家務事

⬙ 實用例句 ·

a real chore 一件苦差事

It was a real chore trying to bath my golden retriever Ginger.

幫我們家的黃金獵犬金吉洗澡真是一件苦差事。

curtain (noun) 窗簾

定義 ► a piece of cloth that is used to cover the window

常用搭配語 ► verb + curtain

open		打開窗簾
draw	**curtain**	拉開窗簾
pull		拉開窗簾

⬙ 實用例句 ·

pushed back the curtain 窗簾往後拉

As soon as I checked in my room, I pushed back the curtain to let the sunshine pour in.

我一進房間，就把窗簾往後拉好讓陽光灑進來。

kitchen (noun) 廚房

定義 ► a place where you can cook

常用搭配語 ► kitchen + noun

	cabinet	廚房櫃子
kitchen	sink	廚房水槽

	utensils	廚房用具
kitchen	foil	廚房鋁箔紙
	waste	廚餘

🔖 實用例句 ·····························

kitchen garden 廚房菜園

There is a kitchen garden on my rooftop, which means I plant and grow fruits and vegetables for my kitchen.

我家屋頂有個廚房菜園，也就是說我種植了一些廚房用的蔬菜和水果。

bedroom (noun) 臥室

定義 ▸ a room used for sleeping or resting

常用搭配語 ▸ verb + bedroom

share		共用一間臥室
convert	**bedroom**	改建臥室
redecorate		重新裝潢臥室

🔖 實用例句 ·····························

scattered over the bedroom 散滿整個臥室

I saw all of his dirty clothes scattered over the bedroom when I entered his room.

當我進入他房間時，髒衣服散滿整個臥室。

Key Expression
情境表達套用語

every nook and cranny 處處

The overseas souvenirs are stuffed with every nook and cranny of my house.

我家到處都是我出國買的戰利品。

Unit 38

Ideas
靈光一現

> Your car runs faster than mine.
> 你的車跑得比較快。

With (the benefit of) hindsight, I should have bought this car.
事後想想，我真該買這部車才對。

---

idea (noun) 主意

定義 ▶ a thought or an opinion about something

常用搭配語 ▶ adj + idea

brilliant		絕佳的主意
wacky	**idea**	詭異的主意
alternative		替代性的主意

◈ 實用例句 •

put my idea into action 想法成真

I just can't find someone whom I can work with to put my idea into action.
我就是想不出來，有誰可以一起合作讓我的想法成真。

think (verb) 想

定義 — to have an idea in your mind

常用搭配語 — think + adv

	carefully	仔細地想
think	hard	想破頭
	miserably	悲慘地想
	thoroughly	全盤地想

🔖 實用例句 ···

I can't help but think of my family first year when I moved to the dorm in college.
當我第一年剛搬進大學宿舍時，我會忍不住想念我的家人。

problem (noun) 問題

定義 — something that is difficult to understand or deal with

常用搭配語 — verb + problem

pose / cause		造成問題
encounter		遇到問題
solve	problem	解決問題
avoid		避免問題
analyze		分析問題

🔖 實用例句 ···

Cash shortage caused a major problem for him to run for his election campaign.
資金短缺造成他開始選舉活動的主要問題。

condition (noun) 狀態

定義 — the state or the way of a thing

常用搭配語 — adj + condition

perfect		完美狀態
pristine	condition	純淨狀態
poor		極差狀態
physical		身體狀態

🗂 實用例句 ··

in excellent condition 極佳的性能狀態

My 8-year Mercedes coupe is still in excellent condition.

我開了 8 年的賓士一直在極佳的性能狀態。

solution (noun) 解決方案

定義 the plan or answer to a problem

常用搭配語 adj + solution

cost-efficient		省錢的解決方案
ideal	solution	理想的解決方案
short-term		短期的解決方案

🗂 實用例句 ··

practical solution 實際解決方案

Everyone was impressed by the practical solution she proposed in the meeting.

大家對她在會議中所提出的實際解決方案印象深刻。

Key Expression
情境表達套用語

with(the benefit of)hindsight 後見之明

With (the benefit of) hindsight, I should have bought this car.

事後想想，我真該買這部車才對。

Journalism & News
新聞業和新鮮事

> The news soon leaked out.
> 這消息很快地洩漏了出去。

The witness leaks the secret to the reporter.
證人洩漏秘密給記者。

report (noun) 報告 / 報導

定義 a written or spoken description of an event or a situation

常用搭配語 adj + report

full		完整的報告 / 導
up-to-date		最新的報告 / 導
in-depth	**report**	深度的報告 / 導
verbal		口頭的報告 / 導
on-the-spot		現場的報告 / 導

實用例句 ·······································

be commissioned to do a report 被委託作報告
Our department was commissioned to do a report on juvenile delinquency.
我們的部門被委託製作一個青少年犯罪的報告。

scandal (noun) 醜聞

定義 ▸ something that is immoral , shocking and unacceptable

常用搭配語 ▸ adj + scandal

nasty		天大的醜聞
national		國家的醜聞
bribery	scandal	收賄的醜聞
political		政治的醜聞
sexual		性醜聞

◈ 實用例句 ····················

a series of scandals 一連串的醜聞
People rally and march on the street to voice their questions and indignation to a series of scandals inside the government.
人們聚集走上街頭，表達憤怒和對政府一連串內部醜聞的疑問。

sexual scandal 性醜聞
The president has received a backlash on social media reporting his sexual scandal.
總統因為他的性醜聞，被社會媒體報導受到反彈。

news (noun) 消息 / 新聞

定義 ▸ information or report of something that has happened

常用搭配語 ▸ adj + news

terrific		天大的好消息 / 新聞
tragic		悲慘的消息 / 新聞
latest		最新的消息 / 新聞
regional		地區的消息 / 新聞
encouraging	news	令人振奮的消息 / 新聞
front-page		頭條 / 頭版消息 / 新聞
exciting		令人興奮的消息 / 新聞
domestic		國內的消息 / 新聞

實用例句 ···

some information in news 新聞的某些資訊

Some information in news could be swayed by media.

新聞的某些資訊（真實性）可能會被媒體所左右。

reporter (noun) 記者

定義 a person who writes or tells people what has happened

常用搭配語 adj + reporter

chief		首席記者
cub		新手記者
investigative	**reporter**	調查記者
freelance		自由記者

實用例句 ···

leaks the secret to the reporter 洩漏秘密給記者

The witness leaks the secret to the reporter.

證人洩漏秘密給記者。

freelance reporter 自由記者

He is now working as a freelance reporter for a Non-Profit Organization.

他現今為一家非營利組織，擔任自由記者的職位。

inquire (verb) 詢問

定義 to ask for more information

常用搭配語 adv + inquire

boldly		大膽地詢問
curiously		好奇地詢問
sarcastically		諷刺地詢問
superficially	**inquire**	膚淺地詢問
bluntly		直言不諱地詢問
officially		正式地詢問

inquired with sweet voice 用撒嬌的聲音詢問

"Could you please spell your name？" she inquired with sweet voice on the phone.

「可以請你把名字拼一次嗎」？她在電話中用撒嬌的聲音詢問。

sarcastically inquired 諷刺地詢問

My ex-boyfriend sarcastically inquired about the reason I got divorced.

我的前男友諷刺地詢問我離婚的原因。

Key Expression
情境表達套用語

celebrity tabloid 名人八卦

Celebrity tabloids are always selling like hot cakes in the UK.

名人八卦在英國像剛出爐的熱蛋糕—超熱賣的。

Unit 40

Knowledge & Ignorance
知識和無知

Math is my favorite.
我喜歡的是數學。

What was your favorite subject when you were in graduate school?
你在研究所的時候最喜歡的科目是哪科？

understand (verb) 瞭解

定義 ➤ to know how something worked or happened

常用搭配語 ➤ adv + understand

fully		完全地瞭解
easy to		容易地了解
hard to	**understand**	很困難去了解
not really to		真的不了解
instinctively		直覺地了解

📚 實用例句 ·······················

didn't understand my question 無法理解我的問題
My coworker didn't understand my question after the presentation.
我的同事在簡報後無法理解我的問題。

intelligent (adj) 聰明

定義 ▸ have ability to learn and understand things easily or solve a difficult problem

常用搭配語 ▸ adv + intelligent

seemingly		似乎看起來聰明
obviously	**intelligent**	明顯地聰明
fairly		相當地聰明
extremely		極度地聰明

◈ 實用例句 ··

the most intelligent person 最聰明的人

He is the most intelligent person that I have ever met.

他是我遇過最聰明的人。

inquisitive (adj) 過問

定義 ▸ ask for information

常用搭配語 ▸ adv + inquisitive

maliciously		惡意地過問
inordinately		過度地好問
relentlessly	**inquisitive**	不斷地過問
impolitely		沒禮貌地過問
highly		高度地好奇

◈ 實用例句 ··

The kid is impolitely inquisitive about the way crippled people move.

那個小孩沒禮貌地過問殘障人士走路的方式。

subject (noun) 科目

定義 ▸ area of study

常用搭配語 ▸ adj + subject

easy		簡單的科目
diffiicult		困難的科目
compulsory	**subject**	必修的科目
optional		選修的科目
specialist		專業科目

實用例句 ·····································

favorite subject 最喜歡的科目

What was your favorite subject when you were in graduate school？

你在研究所的時候最喜歡的科目是哪科？

predict (noun) 預測

定義 ▶ to say that something might happen in the future

常用搭配語 ▶ verb + predict

be able to		能夠預測
be unable to		不能夠預測
be easy to	**predict**	容易預測
be possible to		可能預測
fail to		無法預測

實用例句 ·····································

widely predict 廣泛的預測

The possible result of this election is widely predicted by the internet opinion poll.

這次選舉的可能結果在網路意見投票中廣泛的被預測。

Key Expression
情境表達套用語

who would have the thought that 任誰都沒想過

Who would have the thought that we are actually star dusts?

任誰都沒想過我們其實來自於星塵。

Unit 41 | **Leisure & Hobbies**
休閒嗜好

I can conjure a rabbit out of this hat.
我能從帽子裡變出兔子來。

He has pursued his hobby as amateur magician single-mindedly since the breakup with Marcela.

自從他跟 Marcela 分手後，他就一心一意地投入追求當業餘魔術師的興趣。

pursue (verb) 追求

定義 ▸ try to follow or be involved in an activity

常用搭配語 ▸ adv + pursue

further		進一步追求
still		持續追求
energetically	**pursue**	精力旺盛地追求
doggedly		堅持不斷地追求
effectively		有效果地追求

◈ 實用例句 ·····························

pursued single-mindedly 一心一意地投入

He has pursued his hobby as amateur magician single-mindedly since the breakup with Marcela.

自從他跟 Marcela 分手後，他就一心一意地投入追求當業餘魔術師的興趣。

moment (noun) 時刻

定義　certain point of time, short period of time

常用搭配語　adj + moment

fleeting		霎那時刻
critical		節骨眼
precious		寶貴時刻
awkward		難為情的時刻
difficult	moment	艱難的時刻
perfect		完美的時刻
unguarded		不設防的時刻
historic		歷史性的一刻

實用例句 ·····································

I confessed my love to her in a romantic moment during the candle-lit dinner.
我在燭光晚餐中的浪漫時刻向她表白我的愛意。

activity (noun) 活動

定義　something that is done by a group of people for fun or particular purpose

常用搭配語　adj + activity

social		社交活動
outdoor	activity	戶外活動
group		團體活動
commercial		商業活動

實用例句 ·····································

This parking lot becomes a hive of activity for car lovers on the weekend.
這個停車場週末變成汽車愛好者的活動聚集地。

comfortable (adj) 舒適

定義 ▶ the relaxed feeling of free from worries, and pains

常用搭配語 ▶ verb + comfortable

feel		感覺舒適
look	**comfortable**	看起來舒適
make yourself		別拘謹

實用例句 ·

I think this hotel is comfortable enough to host our wedding guests.
我認為這家旅館夠舒適可以招待我們的婚禮來賓。

hobby (noun) 嗜好

定義 ▶ the activity you pursue outside of your work for fun and relaxation

常用搭配語 ▶ verb + hobby

have		有嗜好
enjoy	**hobby**	享受嗜好樂趣
take up		開始嗜好

實用例句 ·

Have you got any hobbies? 你有任何興趣嗜好嗎？
I take cooking as my favorite hobby.
我把煮菜當作我最愛的嗜好。

Key Expression
情境表達套用語

throw a party 開派對
I plan to throw a party to celebrate my promotion.
我計畫要開個派對來慶祝我的升遷。

Unit
42

Like & Dislike
喜和惡

Your report is due today.
報告今天要交啊！

The new manager is universally disliked in the office.
這新來的經理在辦公室裡顧人怨。

like (verb) 喜歡

定義 ▶ be fond of something

常用搭配語 ▶ adv + like

really		真的喜歡
always	like	一直喜歡
never		從不喜歡
like	a lot	非常喜歡
	better	較喜歡

📚 實用例句 ‧‧

universally like 人見人愛（普遍地喜歡）
I can tell you that this movie is universally liked.
我可以告訴你這部電影是人見人愛。

dislike (verb) 不喜歡

定義 something you don't like

常用搭配語 adv + dislike

simply		單純地不喜歡
intensely	dislike	極度地不喜歡
obviously		明顯地不喜歡
strongly		強烈地不喜歡

◇ 實用例句 ··

universally dislike 顧人怨（普遍地不喜歡）
The new manager is universally disliked in the office.
這新來的經理在辦公室裡顧人怨。

contempt (noun) 不屑 / 輕視

定義 a lack of respect for something or someone

常用搭配語 verb + contempt

have / feel		不屑輕視
develop	contempt	變成輕視
deserve		活該被輕視
hold sb / sth in		對⋯輕視

◇ 實用例句 ··

familiarity breeds contempt 親密生嫌隙
There is a proverb that says familiarity breeds contempt.
諺語說得好：親密生嫌隙。

passion (noun) 熱情

定義 a strong feeling of excitement about someone or doing something

常用搭配語 verb + passion

develop		產生熱情
have	**passion**	有熱情
share		分享熱情
Indulge		沉溺熱情
passion	wane	熱情衰落消失

📚 **實用例句** ....

passion for travelling 對旅行的熱情
My passion for travelling will never wane.
我對旅行的熱情永不減。

tolerate (verb) 忍受

定義 ▸ to allow something to happen

常用搭配語 ▸ verb + tolerate

could / could not		能 / 不能忍受
be unable to		無法忍受
be prepared to	**tolerate**	準備忍受
be willing to		願意忍受
find myself difficult to		我發覺很難忍受

📚 **實用例句** ....

prepared to tolerate 準備去忍受
I 'm not prepared to tolerate his addiction to video games any longer!
我再也不要準備去忍受玩電動玩上癮的他。

🗝 Key Expression
情境表達套用語

of all ages 老少皆愛 / 不分年齡
Disney park is a fabulous place of all ages.
迪士尼樂園是老少皆愛的絕佳地方。

Unit 43 | **Language & Skills**
語言與技能

> I run for 30 minutes daily.
> 我每天跑 30 分鐘。

After a strenuous exercise, I feel like that I am really burning out.
經過吃力的鍛鍊後，我整個覺得我快掛了。

language (noun) 語言

| 定義 | the system of words for communication |

| 常用搭配語 | adj + language |

first / native		第一 / 本地語言
second / foreign		第二 / 外國語言
dead		死去不再使用的語言
local / indigenous		當地說的語言
official	language	官方語言
international		國際語言
body		身體語言
everyday		每天都說的語言
spoken		口語

technical	language	科技 / 技術語
computer		電腦語言

實用例句 ·

minority languages 少數語言

It is sad that some minority languages are dying out due to English predominance around the globe.

據說有些少數語言正在逝去消失中，因為英語獨佔了全球的關係。

skill (noun) 技術 / 技巧

定義 the ability to do something that learned from experience , training or practice

常用搭配語 adj + skill

culinary	skill	烹飪技術
considerable		多才多藝
consummate		完美的技術
poor		技術差
basic		基本技巧
organizational		統整的技巧
problem-solving		解決問題的技巧
study		學習技巧
social		社交技巧

實用例句 ·

extraordinary organizational skill 非凡的協調能力

With her extraordinary organizational skill, the meeting came off without any problems.

有了她的非凡的協調能力，會議很圓滿的成功了。

exercise (noun) 訓練 / 鍛鍊

定義 an activity that is aimed to become healthier and stronger

常用搭配語 adj + exercise

daily		日常練習
regular	**exercise**	持續練習
strenuous		費力的練習
gentle		溫和的練習

verb + exercise

do		作練習
get	**exercise**	從事練習
need		需要鍛鍊
take		從事鍛鍊

⊗ 實用例句 ··

strenuous exercise 吃力的鍛鍊
After a strenuous exercise, I feel like that I am really burning out.
經過吃力的鍛鍊後，我整個覺得我快掛了。

test (noun) 測驗

| 定義 | a series of questions for measuring knowledge and skill |

| 常用搭配語 | adj + test |

aptitude		性向測驗
language oral		語言口語測驗
proficiency		精通度測驗
endurance	**test**	忍耐力測試
placement		分班測驗
driving		駕駛測驗
screen		電腦測驗

⊗ 實用例句 ··

I hate that I have to retake my driving test next week.
我超討厭我下周要重考駕照。

Yay! I aced my test in Math!
耶！我數學考超好的！

vocabulary (noun) 單字

定義 the words that make up a language system

常用搭配語 adj + vocabulary

extensive		延伸性單字
formal		正式的單字
key	vocabulary	關鍵的單字
limited		有限的單字
specialized		專門的單字
technical		技術性的單字

實用例句 ·······································

extensive vocabulary 延伸性單字

It is essential to develop extensive vocabulary to use into your daily situation.

發展延伸性單字好使用於每天的情境是很重要的。

Key Expression
情境表達套用語

day to day conversation 日常交談

HTC requires all the employees to use English in day-to-day conversation.

HTC 要求所有員工在日常交談中都要用英文。

Unit 44

Love & Marriage
愛情與婚姻

I'm in love.
我戀愛了。

He fell in love with Sally instantly on a first date.
他第一次跟 Sally 約會就立刻愛上了她。

love (noun) 愛

定義 ▸ a strong and romantic feeling for a person

常用搭配語 ▸ adj + love

deep		深深的愛
true		真愛
platonic		柏拉圖 (精神式) 之愛
homosexual		同性之愛
maternal	love	母性之愛
unconditional		無條件的愛
unrequited		單一方之愛
eternal		永恆之愛

fall in love 愛上

He fell in love with Sally instantly on a first date.

他第一次跟 Sally 約會就立刻愛上了她。

marriage (noun) 婚姻

定義 ▶ the relationship between a husband and a wife

常用搭配語 ▶ adj + marriage

arranged		由父母安排的婚姻
broken		破碎的婚姻
childless		沒有小孩的婚姻
early / late	**marriage**	早婚 / 晚婚
happy / unhappy		快樂的 / 不快樂的婚姻
previous		前一段婚姻
first / second		第一次 / 再婚
Interracial		跨種族婚姻

marriage is falling apart 婚姻正搖搖欲墜

My marriage is falling apart, as my husband is having office affair with his co-worker.

我的婚姻正搖搖欲墜，因為我老公正跟他公司的同事搞外遇。

arranged marriage 父母安排的婚姻

Arranged marriage still exists in backward countries like India and China.

在印度和中國這種落後國家，由父母親安排的婚姻仍然存在。

wedding (noun) 婚禮

定義 ▶ a ceremony at which two people married each other

常用搭配語 ▶ wedding + noun

	anniversary	結婚周年紀念日
wedding	album	結婚相簿
	guests	婚禮來賓
	day	結婚日
	gown	結婚禮服
	reception	喜宴
	invitation	婚禮邀請
	preparation	結婚準備

實用例句

civil wedding 公證結婚
We have decided to arrange a civil wedding.
我們已經決定要參加公證結婚。

couple (noun) 一對伴侶

定義 ▶ two people or two things that are together

常用搭配語 ▶ adj + couple

infertile		不孕的夫妻
gay		同性戀伴侶
cohabiting	**couple**	同居的伴侶
middle-aged		中年伴侶
newly-wed		新婚的一對

實用例句

newly-wed couples 新婚夫妻
Koh Tao has become one of the honeymoon getaways for newly-wed couples.
濤島已經成為新婚夫妻熱門蜜月地點之一。

romance (noun) 戀情

定義 an activity or relationship that is full of strong emotions

常用搭配語 adj + romance

brief		短暫的戀情
broken		破碎的戀情
teenage		青少年戀情
whirlwind	romance	旋風般 (快速) 的戀情
holiday / vacation		假日 / 渡假戀情 / 浪漫史
weekend		週末的戀情 / 浪漫史

實用例句

broken romance 傷心的戀情

Ted just needs to put himself together and get over that broken romance he had with a beautiful Italian girl.

Ted 真的需要振作自己走出和那個義大利妹妹傷心的戀情。

Key Expression
情境表達套用語

toast for mutual happiness 為我們共同的幸福乾杯

Let us raise our wine glasses and toast for mutual happiness.

讓我們高舉酒杯為我們共同的幸福乾杯吧。

Unit

Meetings & Arrangements
會議和安排

> Meet you at nine sharp tomorrow morning.
> 明天早上 9 點整見哦。

I am calling to confirm the final arrangement for tomorrow's trade show.
我打電話來確認明天商展的最後安排。

reservation (noun) 預訂

定義 ▸ the arrangement to have table or seat to be held for you

常用搭配語 ▸ verb + reservation

confirm		確認預訂
cancel		取消預訂
have	**reservation**	有預訂
make		進行預訂

noun + reservation

airline		班機預訂
hotel	**reservation**	旅館預訂
restaurant		餐廳預訂

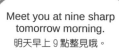

cancel hotel reservation 取消飯店預訂

My old sports injury is acting up again, I have no choice but cancel my hotel reservation for my family's vacation.

我的運動舊傷又開始作怪了，我不得不取消家庭度假計畫中的飯店預訂。

detail (noun) 細節

| 定義 | every tiny part of something |

| 常用搭配語 | verb + detail |

enter		輸入細節
lack in		缺乏細節
find out		找出細節
check	detail	檢查細節
finalize		確定細節
go into		進入細節

◈ **實用例句** •

personal details 個人細節

Enter all the personal details and click the "submit" button.

輸入個人細節後按「提交」鍵。

lack in detail 缺乏細節

This report looks good on paper but lacks in detail.

這報告書面上看起來不錯，但缺乏細節。

arrangement (noun) 安排

| 定義 | a plan for something in the future |

| 常用搭配語 | verb + arrangement |

make		安排
confirm	**arrangement**	確認安排
discuss		討論安排
upset		搞砸了安排

📚 實用例句 ··

final arrangement 最後安排

I am calling to confirm the final arrangement for tomorrow's trade show.

我打電話來確認明天商展的最後安排。

upset arrangement 搞砸

The bad weather upset our arrangement for company retreat.

天氣不佳搞砸了我們公司員工旅遊的安排。

meeting (noun) 會議

定義 ▶ people get together to talk about particular things

常用搭配語 ▶ adj + meeting

face-to-face		面對面會議
introductory		初次會議
urgent	**meeting**	緊急會議
crucial		決定性的會議
follow-up		追蹤會議

📚 實用例句 ··

interminable meeting（冗長）開不完的會議

I am fed up with this interminable meeting.

我真的受夠了這個開不完的會議。

list (noun) 名單

定義 a series of words or numbers in an organized form

常用搭配語 adj + list

complete		完整的名單
comprehensive		綜合的名單
shopping		購物清單
waiting		等待名單
guest	list	來賓名單
alphabetical		按字母排列的名單
reading		閱讀清單
mailing		郵寄名單

實用例句

full list 完整名單

I was asked to make a full list of our local clients.
我被要求製作我們當地客戶的完整名單。

Key Expression
情境表達套用語

something came up 臨時有事

Let us pencil in the meeting for Friday, if something came up, we just make it postponed.
讓我們會議就先定在星期五吧，如果臨時有事我們就把它延後。

Unit 46 | **Memory & Forgetfulness**
記憶和健忘

Oops, it completely slipped my mind!
真糟糕，我全忘了！

I meant to stop by the supermarket on my way home, but it completely slipped my mind.
我本來回家的路上要繞去超市，結果我完全忘了。

remember (verb) 記得

| 定義 | not forget, keep something in your mind |

| 常用搭配語 | adv + remember |

always		一直記得
always	**remember**	一直記得
be-lately		遲來地記得
remember	correctly	正確地記得
suddenly	**remember**	突然地記得
vaguely		模糊地記得

◇ **實用例句** ∙∙∙∙∙∙∙∙∙∙∙∙∙∙∙∙∙∙∙∙∙∙∙∙∙∙∙∙∙∙∙∙∙∙∙∙∙∙

If I remember correctly 如果我沒記錯的話
If I remember correctly, we met in the general meeting last year.
如果我沒記錯的話，我們去年在大會見過面。

memory (noun) 記憶

定義 ▸ something that is remembered and kept in your mind

常用搭配語 ▸ adj + memory

good		記性好
poor	**memory**	記性差
childhood		兒時記憶
photographic		過目不忘

🍃 實用例句 ···

memories came back 回憶湧現

When I visited the place where I grew up, memories came flooding back.
當我再回到我長大的地方，回憶像洪水般湧現。

forget (verb) 忘記

定義 ▸ be unable to remember things or how things happened

常用搭配語 ▸ adv + forget

totally		完全忘記
never		從沒忘記
soon	**forget**	立刻忘記
easily		容易忘記
temporarily		暫時忘記

🍃 實用例句 ···

conveniently forget 索性忘記

I didn't ask and of course; he conveniently forgot to tell me that he is married.
我沒問而他順便索性忘記告訴我他已經結婚了。

remind (verb) 提醒

定義 ▸ to make someone to remember things that they might forget

常用搭配語 ▸ adv + remind

constantly		立刻地提醒
repeatedly	**remind**	反覆地提醒
gently / nicely		溫和地提醒

📚 實用例句 ・・・

remind me of 讓我想到

The way you smiled reminded me of my ex-girlfriend.

你的燦爛笑容讓我想到我前女朋友。

note (noun) 字條說明

定義 ▶ a short piece of writing

常用搭配語 ▶ adj + note

love		愛情宣言
ransom		勒索字條
thank-you	**note**	感謝字條
hand-written		親筆說明
quick		快速註記

📚 實用例句 ・・・

leave a love note 留下充滿愛意的字條

I left a love note to my wife in the kitchen to say that I loved the breakfast she made.

我留下充滿愛意的字條，告訴我老婆我超愛她作的早餐。

🔑 Key Expression
情境表達套用語

It completely slipped my mind. 我完全忘了。

I meant to stop by the supermarket on my way home, but it completely slipped my mind.

我本來回家的路上要繞去超市，結果我完全忘了。

Unit 47

Money & Finance
金錢與財務

It's much easier to get into debt than to get out of debt.
無債一身輕，欠債要人命。

I have got to pay off my debt in two years.
我得要兩年內還清我的債務。

money (noun) 金錢

定義	a coin or bill which is used to buy something

常用搭配語	adj + money

easy		容易賺的錢
taxpayer's	**money**	納稅人的錢
pocket		零用錢
counterfeit		假錢偽鈔

實用例句 ·····················

make big money 賺大錢
You can make big money as a top racing car driver.
當一個頂尖的賽車手可以賺大錢。

income (noun) 收入

定義 ▸ the amount of money you received from work

常用搭配語 ▸ adj + income

low		低收入
average		平均收入
above-average	income	中上收入
pre-tax		未稅收入
retirement		退休收入

◈ **實用例句** ···

personal income 個人（私下）收入

I actually have personal income on top of my current job as an English teacher.
我除了正職的英文老師外其實還有個人收入。

payment (noun) 付款款項

定義 ▸ an amount of money that you have to pay

常用搭配語 ▸ adj + payment

early		提早付款
late	payment	延遲付款
full / part		全額 / 部份付款
immediate		立即付款

◈ **實用例句** ···

payment for work 薪水款項

I won't get my payment for work until next week, but my rent is due this Friday!
我要下星期才拿的到薪水款項，但是我的房租這星期五就到期了。

debt (noun) 債務

定義 ▸ a person owed someone something, usually money

常用搭配語 ▸ adj + debt

crippling		使人破產的債務
huge	debt	龐大的債務
gambling		賭博的債務
overdue		延遲未付的債務

實用例句 ∙∙

pay off debt 還清債務

I have got to pay off my debt in two years.

我得要兩年內還清我的債務。

tax (noun) 稅

定義 the amount of money that you paid to the government

常用搭配語 adj + tax

car / vehicle		汽車 / 車輛稅
road	tax	道路使用稅
import		進口稅
fuel		燃料稅

實用例句 ∙∙

set off against tax 抵稅

Claims for charitable donation can be set off against tax.

提報慈善捐款可以抵稅。

Key Expression
情境表達套用語

cost of living 生活開銷

The cost of living in Taipei is getting higher and higher.

台北的生活開銷是愈來愈高了。

Unit 48

Moods & Feelings
心情與感受

> I never lie!
> 我從不說謊的。

My gut feeling is that he is a liar!
我的直覺告訴我他根本是個騙子！

mood (noun) 心情

定義 the way you feel

常用搭配語 adj + mood

bullish		樂觀心情
pensive	**mood**	心事重重
changing		心情陰晴不定
public		大眾觀感

📚 實用例句 ·

No one could keep up her constantly changing mood.
沒人受得了她的心情說變就變。

She has been in a bullish mood about the future of her company.
她對她公司的前景一直保持樂觀的心情看待。

feeling (noun) 感受

定義	the emotion you feel

常用搭配語 —— adj + feeling

mixed		五味雜陳
general		普遍的感受
gut	**feeling**	直覺
wonderful		美好的感受

實用例句 ·······································

gut feeling 直覺

My gut feeling is that he is a liar!
我的直覺告訴我他根本是個騙子！

rage (noun) 怒氣

定義	great anger

常用搭配語 —— adj + rage

blind		盲目的生氣
suppressed		壓抑的怒氣
jealous	**rage**	忌妒的怒氣
drunken		酒醉失控

實用例句 ·······································

got in a rage 暴怒

She got in a rage when she heard someone badmouthed in her back.
她一聽到有人在背後說她壞話讓她暴怒。

calm (verb) 鎮靜

定義	no worry or anger

常用搭配語 —— adv + calm

outwardly		表面上地鎮靜
perfectly	calm	超級鎮靜
relatively		相對地鎮靜
strangely		奇怪地鎮靜

實用例句 ···

seems pretty calm 似乎相當鎮靜
She seems pretty calm about the news of office downsizing.
她對部門縮減的消息似乎相當鎮靜。

grin (noun) 笑

定義 ▶ smile and show your teeth

常用搭配語 ▶ adj + grin

goofy		古怪的笑
impish	grin	頑皮的一笑
sheepish		緬腆的笑
lopsided		撇嘴一笑

實用例句 ···

grin and bear it 逆來順受
There isn't really much you can make it better and I guess you will have to grin and bear it.
你真的對這是一點辦法都沒有，我看你也只能逆來順受撐下去了。

Key Expression
情境表達套用語

keep your temper 不生氣
It is so hard to keep your temper when you come home and see a big mess around.
當你回家看到家裡超亂，真的很難不生氣。

Movement
動作

> Go away!
> 走開！

I scare mice to death, they make my flesh creep!
我怕老鼠怕死了，牠們讓我起雞皮疙瘩！

walk (noun) 步行

| 定義 | move and make a trip on foot |

| 常用搭配語 | adj + walk |

romantic		浪漫的步行
nature		在大自然步行
charity		慈善步行
brisk		輕快行走
hard / strenuous	walk	吃力的行走
5-minute		五分鐘的步行
brief		短暫的步行
after-dinner		晚餐後的步行
long-distance		長途的步行
tightrope		走鋼索

🔖 實用例句 ••

walking disaster 活災難
You are truly a walking disaster!
你真是人見人倒楣！

run (noun) 跑步 / 測試

定義 to take faster steps than walk

常用搭配語 adj + run

8-mile		8 哩的跑步
school		接送小孩
training	run	跑步訓練
print-		書一次印刷的數量
trial-		試用測試

🔖 實用例句 ••

to do school run 學校接送小孩
Excuse me, I really need to get going. It's my turn to do school run today.
不好意思，我得走了，今天輪到我要去學校接送小孩。

training run 跑步訓練
I'll be doing more exercise and training run in a couple of weeks.
在接下來的幾個禮拜，我會做更多運動和跑步訓練。

wander (verb) 遊蕩

定義 to walk around without any clear plan

常用搭配語 adv + wander

simply		單純地遊蕩
slowly		慢慢地遊蕩
aimlessly	wander	漫無目的地遊蕩
happily		開心地遊蕩
freely		自在地遊蕩

wandering **around** 到處晃
I enjoy wandering around without plan sometimes.
我有時真的很喜歡不設限的到處晃。

creep (verb) 爬行

定義 to move slowly and quietly to avoid being discovered

常用搭配語 adv + creep

slowly		慢慢地爬
secretly		偷偷地爬
quietly	creep	安靜地爬
stealthily		躡手躡腳地

◇ **實用例句** ••

make my flesh creep 讓我起雞皮疙瘩
I scare mice to death, they make my flesh creep!
我怕老鼠怕死了，牠們讓我起雞皮疙瘩！

creeping **slowly** 慢慢地爬
The snail is creeping slowly along the leave after the rain.
雨後，蝸牛慢慢地沿著樹葉爬上去。

wave (verb) 招手

定義 movement of your hand

常用搭配語 adj + wave

cheery		開心愉快的招手
friendly		友善的招手
farewell	wave	道別的招手
quick		快速的招手
vigorous		有精神的招手

gave me a cheery wave 愉快地向我招手
He gave me a cheery wave as soon as I walked into the lobby.
當我一走進大廳他立刻愉快地向我招手。

farewell wave 道別的揮手
She cried and gave me a farewell wave in the train station.
她在車站哭著並且跟我道別揮揮手。

Key Expression
情境表達套用語

I'd better dash. 我得閃了。
I'd better dash or I will miss the bus.
我得快閃不然我會坐不到公車。

Music & Dance
音樂和舞蹈

It is common that my mom walked away with a medal in every singing contest.
我老媽每次參加歌唱比賽都輕鬆抱走獎牌是家常便飯的事。

music (noun) 音樂

定義 arrangement of sounds made by musical instruments for singing or arts

常用搭配語 adj + music

light		輕音樂
background		背景音樂
film	music	電影音樂
theme		主題音樂
folk		民族音樂

 實用例句 •

turn that music down 音樂轉小聲點
Would you please turn that music down, it is too loud to talk to my friend.
拜託你把音樂轉小聲點，我無法和我朋友說話。

dance (noun) 舞蹈

定義 ► a series of movements of your body

常用搭配語 ► adj + dance

traditional		傳統舞蹈
ritual		儀式舞蹈
ballroom		國際標準舞
folk		民族舞蹈
lively	dance	生動舞蹈
slow		慢舞
rain		求雨舞蹈
mating		求偶舞蹈

實用例句

sit out the dance 坐在一旁不參加舞蹈演出
I have to sit out the dance as I just sprained my right ankle.
我必須坐在一旁不參加舞蹈演出,因為我剛剛扭傷了右腳踝。

sing (verb) 歌唱

定義 ► make sounds with music

常用搭配語 ► adv + sing

happily		開心地歌唱
gently	sing	溫和地歌唱
loudly		大聲地歌唱
sing	live	現場歌唱
	together	一起合唱

實用例句

sings me a love song 唱了一首情歌給我聽
She has me in her arms and sings me a love song.
她抱我在懷中並唱了一首情歌給我聽。

singing **happily** 盡情高歌

I always enjoy singing happily in the choir.
在合唱團裡，我總是能盡情高歌。

performance (noun) 演出

定義 ▶ how well people do something

常用搭配語 ▶ adj + performance

live		現場演出
cameo		客串演出
solo	**performance**	獨自演出
public		公開演出
professional		專業演出

實用例句 ···

live performance 現場演出
The live performance didn't come up to my expectation.
這個現場演出並沒有我期待的好。

professional performance 專業演出
Her professional performance earned the standing ovation for as long as 3 minutes.
她的專業演出讓她贏得長達 3 分鐘的起立鼓掌。

artist (noun) 藝術家

定義 ▶ someone who performs arts

常用搭配語 ▶ adj + artist

amateur		業餘的藝術家
struggling		苦苦掙扎的藝術家
talented	**artist**	有才華的藝術家
self-taught		無師自通的藝術家
well-known		著名的藝術家

famous graffiti artist 知名的塗鴉藝術家
The government commissioned a famous graffiti artist to paint the subway.
政府委託一個知名的塗鴉藝術家彩繪地下鐵。

struggling artist 窮困掙扎的畫家
Van Gogh was a struggling artist before his death, he would never ever imagine the future surreal prices of his paintings.
梵谷生前是個窮困掙扎的畫家，他絕對想不到他死後，畫作會飆到天價。

Key Expression
情境表達套用語

walk away with a medal 輕鬆抱走獎牌
It is common that my mom walked away with a medal in every singing contest.
我老媽每次參加歌唱比賽都輕鬆抱走獎牌是家常便飯的事。

Nature & Environment
自然與環境

100% Natural
百分之百天然

The ingredients they used are completely natural.
他們所使用的材料皆完全天然。

natural (adj) 天然的 / 自然的

定義 ▶ not made by human

常用搭配語 ▶ natural + noun

natural	gas	天然氣
	childbirth	自然生產
	disaster	自然災害
	history	自然歷史
	cause	自然原因
	language	自然語言
	resource	天然資源

實用例句 ···

completely natural 完全天然
The ingredients they used are completely natural.
他們所使用的材料皆完全天然。

environment (noun) 環境

定義 the condition of air , water and place where people and animals live

常用搭配語 adj + environment

global		全球的環境
friendly		友善的環境
favorable		叫人喜愛的環境
urban	**environment**	都市環境
home		居家環境
cultural		文化環境
workplace		工作環境
educational		教育環境

實用例句 ···

rural environment 鄉下環境
There are more and more people living in rural environment instead of urban one.
有愈來愈多的人住在鄉下環境而不是都市環境了。

landscape (noun) 景色

定義 a huge area of land, especially in countryside

常用搭配語 adj + landscape

bleak		荒涼的景色
dramatic		驚心動魄的景色
lunar	**landscape**	月球的景色
rocky		崎嶇的景色
rural		鄉野的景色

rural landscape 鄉野景致

The rural landscape here is taking my breath away.

這一番鄉野景致美到讓我嘆為觀止。

species (noun) 物種

| 定義 | a set of animals and plants |

| 常用搭配語 | adj + species |

endangered		瀕危物種
extinct		絕種的物種
related		相關的物種
rare		稀有的物種
native	species	本土的物種
living		現有的物種
common		一般的物種
different		不同的物種
dominant		主要的物種

◇ **實用例句** ・・

animals and plants species 動植物物種

Our country is rich in many different animals and plants species.

我們國家動植物物種生態豐富。

native species 本土物種

Teachers should educate students about how important these native species are to us.

老師應教育學生認識本土物種，它們對我們來說是很重要的。

habitat (noun) 棲地

| 定義 | the natural environment where animals live |

| 常用搭配語 | adj + habitat |

coastal		海岸的棲地
important		重要的棲地
natural	**habitat**	天然的棲地
threatened		受威脅的棲地
wetland		溼地棲地
wildlife		野生動物棲地

 實用例句 ··

natural habitats 天然棲地

The natural habitats for polar rare sea birds are continuously depleting.

稀有極地海鳥的天然棲地正逐漸消失中。

Key Expression
情境表達套用語

the flora and fauna 動植物

Brasil is the paradise for tropical flora and fauna.

巴西這個國家是熱帶動植物的天堂。

Numbers & Statistics

數字與數據

> The number goes to 19 and 37.
> 得獎的號碼是 19、37。

The winning numbers for lottery today are 19 and 37.
今天樂透的得獎數字為 19 和 37。

number (noun) 數字

定義 ➤ a unit that forms part of the system of counting and calculating

常用搭配語 ➤ adj + number

even		偶數字
odd		奇數字
lucky / unlucky	**number**	幸運 / 不幸運數字
prime		質數
random		隨機數字
winning		得獎數字

 實用例句 ··

winning number 得獎數字

The winning numbers for lottery today are 19 and 37.
今天樂透的得獎數字為 19 和 37。

percent (noun) 百分比

定義 ▸ symbol as %, number out of every 100

常用搭配語 ▸ verb + percent* 注意此發音

account for		說明百分比
contain	**percent**	包含百分比
increase		增加百分比
devalue		百分比貶值

🔖 實用例句 ···

40% (percent) of people 百分之 40 的人

Only 40% of people in Taiwan earned a million per year from their job.

在台灣只有百分之 40 的人工作年薪有百萬。

estimate (noun) 估計

定義 ▸ to guess the value of something

常用搭配語 ▸ adj + estimate

accurate		正確的估計
current		現在的估計
cost		成本估計
early		先前的估計
rough	**estimate**	粗略的估計
reliable		可信的估計
optimistic		樂觀的估計
unofficial		非正式的估計

🔖 實用例句 ···

ballpark estimate 大約的估計

Our client asks us to come up with the ballpark estimate for this building project.

我們的客戶要求對此建案提出大約的估計。

cost estimate 成本估算

The cost estimate of this project will amount to a little over thirty thousand USD.

這個專業的成本估算，總共約將超過 3 萬美金。

rate (noun) 比率 / 速度

定義 ▶ the speed or frequency at which something happens or changes

常用搭配語 ▶ adj + rate

alarming		令人吃驚的速度
growth		成長率
inflation		通貨膨脹率
expected		期待比率
marriage / divorce	rate	結婚 / 離婚率
accident / crime		意外 / 犯罪率
success / failure		成功 / 失敗率
seasonally-adjusted		季節性調整率
unemployment		失業率

◈ 實用例句 ‧‧‧‧‧‧‧‧‧‧‧‧‧‧‧‧‧‧‧‧‧‧‧‧‧‧‧‧‧‧‧‧‧‧‧‧‧

unemployment rate 失業率

The unemployment rate is rising at a shocking pace this month.

這個月失業率以驚人的速度升高中。

possibility (noun) 可能性

定義 ▶ the chance that something would happen or become true

常用搭配語 ▶ adj + possibility

further		進一步可能性
future	possibility	未來可能性
strong		強烈可能性
various		各種的可能性

interesting		有趣的可能性
endless	**possibility**	無數的可能性
faint		微弱的可能性
practical		實際可能性

 實用例句 ··

risk the possibility 冒風險

I can't afford to risk the possibility of losing money.

我可擔不起冒這可能賠錢的風險。

Key Expression
情境表達套用語

keep track of 確認跟得上

I read news to keep track of current issues.

我閱讀新聞好跟得上現在社會狀況。

Unit 53

Opinion & Expression
意見與表達

> I really appreciate the support from my family.
> 感謝家人的支持。

Things turned out OK with my family's moral support.
有了我家人的精神支持，事情變順利了。

opinion (noun) 意見

定義 a thought or idea about someone or something

常用搭配語 adj + opinion

honest		誠實的意見
personal		個人的意見
subjective		主觀的意見
objective	opinion	客觀的意見
majority / minority		多數 / 少數的意見
mixed		眾多的意見

🍃 實用例句 ·

ask for my honest opinion 問我的誠實意見

If you ask for my honest opinion, I think you shouldn't buy that product.
如果你是要問我的誠實意見的話，我認為你不應該買那產品。

personal opinion 個人意見

In my personal opinion, citizens in Taipei should be able to take bus for free.
就我個人意見而言，台北市民應可免費搭乘公車。

express (verb) 表達

定義 ▶ to be able to show your feeling, fact or opinion

常用搭配語 ▶ express + adv

	cogently	強而有力地表達
	fully	完整地表達
express	openly	公開地表達
	precisely	精準地表達
	well	很會表達

◇ 實用例句 ····························

hard to express 很難表達
I find it hard to express how I really feel right now.
我發現如何表達我現在的感受很難。

convinced (adj) 說服

定義 ▶ to say something to make someone believe it is true

常用搭配語 ▶ adv + convinced

deeply		深深地說服
not fully	**convinced**	沒有完全說服
increasingly		逐漸地說服
half		一半說服

◇ 實用例句 ····························

only half convinced 半信半疑
I am still only half convinced.
我還是半信半疑。

support (noun) 支持

定義 ▸ to encourage or give help to someone or something

常用搭配語 ▸ adj + support

direct / indirect		直接 / 間接的支持
long-term		長期的支持
personal		個人的支持
mutual	support	互相的支持
moral		道義上 精神支持
technical		技術支援
wholehearted		真心誠意的支持

◇ 實用例句 ·

moral support 精神支持

Things turned out OK with my family's moral support.

有了我家人的精神支持，事情變順利了。

technical support 技術支援

My success won't be possible without the technical support from my team.

如果沒有團隊的技術支援，我是沒可能會成功的。

confidence (noun) 自信

定義 ▸ to have belief in yourself

常用搭配語 ▸ adj + confidence

increasing		增加的自信
sublime		超強的自信
extra	confidence	多一點的自信
social		社交自信
absolute		絕對的自信

great		很有自信
renewed	**confidence**	重新燃起的自信
public		公眾信心

實用例句 ·····························

lack of confidence 缺乏自信
The biggest problem for her is lack of confidence.
她最大的問題就是缺乏自信。

give me extra confidence 讓我更有自信
Passing English test gave me extra confidence in speaking English.
通過英文考試讓我更有自信說英文。

Key Expression
情境表達套用語

personally speaking 就我個人而言
Personally speaking, I don't think this job is rewarding.
就我個人而言，我不認為這工作有意義（有回報）。

Personal life
個人生活

A candle lights others and consumes itself
蠟燭燃燒自己，照亮別人。

She works as a part-time volunteer in an orphanage on weekends.
她每個周末都會去孤兒院當兼職義工。

age (noun) 年齡 / 年紀

| 定義 | how old a person is |

| 常用搭配語 | adj + age |

young		年輕時期
middle		中年時期
school	age	學生時期
working		工作時期
voting		投票年齡

📚 實用例句 •••••••••••••••••••••••••••••••••••••

at my age 在我這年紀的時候
My dad told me that he already started investment at my age.
我老爸說他在我這年紀的時候就開始投資了。

youth (noun) 青春

定義 → the time when you are young

常用搭配語 → adj + youth

early		青春時期
lost	youth	失落的青春
misspent		虛度的青春
unhappy		不快樂的青春

◇ 實用例句 ....

idled my youth away 虛擲了我的青春

My biggest regret is that I idled my youth away.

我最大的遺憾就是我虛擲了我的青春,一無所獲。

retirement (noun) 退休

定義 → to leave your job and stop working

常用搭配語 → adj + retirement

early		提早退休
active	retirement	活躍的退休
happy		快樂的退休
enforced		被迫的退休

◇ 實用例句 ....

Spending my retirement 度過退休

Spending my retirement in Europe is my dream.

在歐洲度過退休是我的夢想。

volunteer (noun) 義工

定義 → a person is will to help the others without being forced or paid

常用搭配語 → adj + volunteer

full-time / part time		全職 / 兼職義工
dedicated	**volunteer**	奉獻的義工
trained		受過訓練的義工
unpaid		不支薪的義工

實用例句

part-time volunteer 兼職義工
She works as a part-time volunteer in an orphanage on weekends.
她每個周末都會去孤兒院當兼職義工。

life (noun) 一生

定義　a personal experience and period between birth and death

常用搭配語　phrases + life

all my / your / his/her		終其你 / 我 / 他的一生
a phase in your		人生的一個階段
late in	**life**	晚年
the love of my		我一生的愛
The rest of my		餘生

實用例句

I don't plan to spend my whole life here, I want to explore how big the world is!
我可不想一輩子待在這裡，我要去探索這世界有多大！

Key Expression
情境表達套用語

pull yourself up by your own bootstraps 白手起家
Apparently, he pulled himself up by his own bootstraps. He doesn't rely on anybody.
很明顯地，他是白手起家不靠任何人。

Unit 55 | **People appearance**
人體樣貌

> My toothache is gone now!
> 牙齒不痛了！

I had one cavity out from the dentist.
我去牙醫那邊拔了一顆蛀牙。

skin (noun) 皮膚

| 定義 | the thing layer which covers a person |

| 常用搭配語 | adj + skin |

dark		黑皮膚
pale		蒼白的皮膚
tanned		曬黑的皮膚
healthy	skin	健康的皮膚
smooth		光滑的皮膚
puffy		水腫的皮膚
winkled		有皺紋的皮膚

◈ 實用例句 ·

sensitive skin 敏感的肌膚

The lotion I bought really irritated my sensitive skin.
我買的那罐乳液真的會刺激我敏感的肌膚。

tanned skin 曬成古銅色
Getting tanned skin at the beach is popular in the western.
去海邊曬成古銅色的肌膚在西方超流行的。

hair (noun) 頭髮

定義 a covering of hairs on a person's head and body

常用搭配語 adj + hair

gray		灰白髮
glossy		滑順的秀髮
straight		直髮
wavy	hair	波浪捲髮
greasy		油膩的頭髮
sleek		漂亮秀髮
windswept		被風吹動的秀髮

實用例句

got hair cut 剪了頭髮
He got his hair cut on the way home from work.
他下班回家的路上去剪了頭髮。

appearance (noun) 外表

定義 the way a person looks

常用搭配語 adj + appearance

attractive		迷人的外表
disheveled		亂糟糟的外表
overall	appearance	整體外觀
personal		個人儀容

general		一般儀容
handsome	**appearance**	帥氣外表
youthful		年輕外表
striking		引人注目的外表

◈ 實用例句 ···

put in an appearance 露臉

I really don't feel like going to that stupid party, but I think I'd better put in an apperarance.

我實在不想去那愚蠢的派對，不過我想我最好還是露一下臉就好。

tooth(單數) / teeth(複數) (noun) 牙

> **定義** the hard and white objects in your mouth for biting and chewing food

> **常用搭配語** adj + teeth

crooked		歪牙
even		整齊的牙
decayed		蛀牙
gappy	**teeth**	有齒縫的牙
missing		缺牙
pearl-white		雪白的牙
yellow		黃牙

◈ 實用例句 ···

decayed tooth 蛀牙

I had one decayed tooth out from the dentist.

我去牙醫那邊拔了一顆蛀牙。

weight (noun) 體重

> **定義** the amount of a person weighs

> **常用搭配語** weight + noun

weight	control	體重控制
	gain	體重增加
	loss	體重減輕
	problem	體重問題

實用例句

watch my weight 注意我的體重
I 'll pass the dessert, I need to watch my weight.
甜點我跳過不吃了，因為我要注意我的體重。

losing weight 減重
The key to losing weight is to take regular exercise and eat healthy.
減重的關鍵在於規律的運動和健康的飲食。

Key Expression
情境表達套用語

make a good impression 留下良好印象
It is essential to make a good impression on the first met.
第一次碰面留下良好印象是很重要的。

Unit 56 | Politics
政治

> The matter will be decided by vote .
> 由投票決定這件事。

This law should be ratified by popular vote.
這個法律透過公民投票應該被修改。

election (noun) 選舉

定義 the activity that people vote for someone to do the official job

常用搭配語 election + noun

election	candidate	選舉候選人
	defeat / victory	選舉失利 / 勝利
	fraud	選舉詐欺
	promise	選舉承諾

📚 實用例句 ·······················

run-up to the presidential election 總統選舉的最後階段
Everyone is way busy during the run-up to the presidential election.
大家在總統選舉的最後階段都忙到不行。

vote (verb) 投票

定義 ▸ to voice your choice or opinion by marking on a piece of paper or raising hands

常用搭配語 ▸ adj + vote

democratic		民主投票
majority		多數投票
valid / invalid	**vote**	有效 / 無效投票
narrow		票數拉鋸
unanimous		票投一致

◈ 實用例句 ·

popular vote 公民投票
This law should be ratified by popular vote.
這個法律透過公民投票應該被修改。

enforcement (noun) 執法

定義 ▸ to make people obey the law

常用搭配語 ▸ adj + enforcement

effective		有效執法
strict	**enforcement**	嚴格執法
legal		法規執法
police		警察執法

◈ 實用例句 ·

tougher enforcement 更強硬的執法
The union calls for tougher enforcement of human trafficking.
聯合國要求對人口販賣應要有更強硬的執法。

government (noun) 政府

定義 ▸ the group of people who officially run the country

常用搭配語 ▸ adj + government

local		當地政府
military	**government**	軍方政府
puppet		傀儡政府
transitional		過渡政府

實用例句 ·····························

corrupt government 貪汙腐敗的政府

The political dissidents plan to topple this corrupt government.

政治的異議分子計畫要推翻這個貪汙的政府。

candidate (noun) 候選人

定義 ➤ a person who is trying to get a job or elected position

常用搭配語 ➤ adj + candidate

democratic		民主的候選人
ideal		理想的候選人
unsuitable	**candidate**	不適任的候選人
potential		有希望的候選人
presidential		總統候選人

實用例句 ·····························

the first female presidential candidate 第一位女性總統候選人

She will stand as the first female presidential candidate for DPP.

她將成為 DPP 第一位女性總統候選人。

🔑 Key Expression
情境表達套用語

won a landslide victory 贏得壓倒性的勝利

Most people aren't surprised that DPP won a landslide victory in primary election.

大部分的人對 DPP 在初選贏得壓倒性的勝利並不感到驚訝。

Problem & Solution

問題和解決方案

> I know I can find the answer.
> 我知道我可以找出答案。

I just hope that I can overcome the setback on my job soon.

我只希望我能快點克服我工作上的挫折。

difficulty (noun) 困難

定義   something is hard to do or understand

常用搭配語   adj + difficulty

learning		學習困難
financial	difficulty	財務困難
technical		技術困難
major		主要困難

◈ 實用例句 ·····························

practical difficulty 實在很難的困難

I am glad that I have this practical difficulty solved.

我很高興我把這實在很難的困難解決了。

situation (noun) 情況

定義 ▸ the fact that happens to someone at certain time and place

常用搭配語 ▸ adj + situation

actual		實際的情況
complex	**situation**	複雜的情況
overall		全面的情況
unpleasant		使人討厭的情況

實用例句 ·····························

a win-win situation 雙贏的居面
We are all out for creating a win-win situation.
我們都致力於要創造一個雙贏的居面。

solve (verb) 解決

定義 ▸ to get an answer to problem

常用搭配語 ▸ adv + solve

easily		輕易地解決
partly		部分地解決
quickly	**solve**	快速地解決
finally		終於解決
never		從沒解決過

實用例句 ·····························

completely solve 徹底解決
This tricky problem has been completely solved.
這棘手的問題已經被徹底解決了。

setback (noun) 挫折

定義 ▸ something that prevents someone from success

常用搭配語 ▸ adj + setback

financial		財務不順
unexpected	**setback**	未料到的挫折
temporary		暫時的挫折

實用例句

I just hope that I can overcome the setback on my job soon.
我只希望我能快點克服我工作上的挫折。

measure (noun) 措施 / 手段

定義 action to deal with the problem

常用搭配語 adj + measure

corrective		改正措施
necessary	**measure**	必要的手段
tough		強硬的手段
urgent		緊急措施

實用例句

cost-cutting measure 削減成本措施
Cost-cutting measure has been taken to stay in the budget.
削減成本措施啟動才能不超過預算。

Key Expression
情境表達套用語

It puts me in a very difficult position 不知如何是好
The current situation just puts me in a very difficult position.
現在的情況讓我不知如何是好。

Personality & Style

個性與風格

> All of my friends must be jealous.
> 姐妹們一定很羨慕我。

I'm into public display of affection with my boyfriend.
我跟我男朋友超愛放閃的。

personality (noun) 個性

定義 ▶ the way you behave, feel and think

常用搭配語 ▶ adj + personality

bright		聰明快樂的個性
charming		迷人的個性
dominant	**personality**	主導的個性
multiple		多重人格

◈ 實用例句 ·····

personality clash 個性不合
There is a personality clash between me and Helen.
Helen 和我個性不合。

childhood (noun) 童年

the time when you were a child

常用搭配語 ━━ adj + childhood

happy / unhappy		快樂 / 不快樂的童年
normal	**childhood**	正常普通的童年
lonely		孤單的童年
traumatic		受創的童年

◈ 實用例句 ······························

traumatic childhood 受創的童年

His traumatic childhood made his personality slightly distorted.

他那精神受創的童年讓他的人格有點扭曲。

sensitivity (noun) 感受力 / 敏銳度

定義 ━━ the ability to understand what the others need

常用搭配語 ━━ adj + sensitivity

extreme		絕佳的感受力
great	**sensitivity**	良好的敏銳度
increased		增加的敏銳度

◈ 實用例句 ······························

lacks sensitivity 缺乏反應敏銳力

The problem is that she lacks sensitivity in dealing with conflict.

問題是她對處理衝突缺乏反應敏銳力。

background (noun) 背景

定義 ━━ a person's family and experience of education, work and life

常用搭配語 ━━ adj + background

deprived		資源不足的背景
privileged	**background**	特權背景
middle class		中產階級背景
educational		教育背景

實用例句 ··

broad educational background 廣泛的教育背景
Having a broad educational background helps you open the door to jobs.
擁有廣泛的教育背景有助你打開求職大門。

affection (noun) 喜愛

定義 ▶ a feeling of liking someone or something

常用搭配語 ▶ adj + affection

deep		深深的喜愛
genuine	**affection**	真正的喜愛
strong		強烈的喜愛
mutual		雙方的喜愛

實用例句 ··

public display of affection 公開示愛
I'm into public display of affection with my boyfriend.
我跟我男朋友超愛放閃的。

🔑 Key Expression
情境表達套用語

What's he / she like？ 他／她是如何？（指個性上）
What's your new boyfriend like？
你的男朋友是什麼樣的人？

Questions
問題一籮筐

Thanks.
Please step aside.
謝謝，請讓開。

He refused to answer any personal questions.
他拒絕回答任何私人問題。

question (noun) 問題

定義 ── a sentence you ask to get more information

常用搭配語 ── adj + question

direct		直接的問題
tricky	**question**	棘手的問題
relevant		相關的問題
personal		私人的問題

實用例句 ····································

personal questions 私人問題
He refused to answer any personal questions.
他拒絕回答任何私人問題。

hint (noun) 提示

定義 ► something you did or show indirectly what you want

常用搭配語 ► adj + hint

strong		強烈的提示
subtle	hint	微妙的提示
tantalizing		吊人胃口的暗示

實用例句

get the hint 懂暗示

Can't you get the hint from me and leave me alone ?!

欸！難道你不懂我的暗示嗎？我一個人靜靜好嗎！

intelligence (noun) 智能

定義 ► the ability to learn, understand and react

常用搭配語 ► adj + intelligence

high		高智能
limited	intelligence	智能不足
average		一般智能
artificial		人工智慧

實用例句

intelligence is limited 能力不夠

I think his intelligence is limited in dealing with this matter.

我想他的能力不能解決這問題。

answer (noun) 答案

定義 ► the reaction to questions, activities

常用搭配語 ► verb + answer

have / know		找到答案
look for	**answer**	尋求答案
come up with		想出對策
give		問答 / 解答

實用例句 ······························

perfect answer 完美答案
I think I have found the perfect answer to your question.
我想我已經找到回答你問題的完美答案了。

puzzled (adj) 迷惑

定義　　a feeling of experiencing difficulty

常用搭配語　　verb + puzzled

become		變得迷惑
feel	**puzzled**	覺得迷惑
seem		似乎迷惑
remain		依然迷惑

實用例句 ······························

remain puzzled 依然迷惑
I still remain puzzled by the words he said.
我對他說的話依然很迷惑。

Key Expression
情境表達套用語

out of curiosity 出於好奇心
He asked about my family out of curiosity.
他出於好奇心的問了我家狀況。

Relationships & Rearing kids
關係與養小孩

Happily remarried.
快樂地再婚。

She has got 2 children since she remarried to her second husband.
從她再婚嫁了第二任老公，她一共有 2 個小孩。

parent (noun) 父母

定義 ▸ a father or a mother

常用搭配語 ▸ adj + parent

single		單親父母
foster		代養父母
biological	**parent**	親生父母
over-protective		過度保護的父母
indulgent		溺愛的父母

◇ 實用例句 ••••••••••••••••••••••••••••••••

Not all parents are right!
天下也有不是父母！

relationship (noun) 關係

定義 ▶ the way you connect with people and life around you

常用搭配語 ▶ adj + relationship

harmonious		和諧的關係
intimate		親密的關係
stable	relationship	穩定的關係
physical		肉體的關係
interpersonal		人際關係
one-to-one		一對一的關係

◈ 實用例句 ·

stable relationship 穩定的關係

I am not married, but I am in a stable relationship.

我未婚但是我有一段穩定發展的戀情。

child (noun) 孩子

定義 ▶ a boy or a girl

常用搭配語 ▶ adj + child

well-behaved		行為良好的孩子
wayward	child	任性的小孩
neglected		被忽略的小孩
illegitimate		私生子

◈ 實用例句 ·

has / have got 2 children 有 2 個小孩

She has got 2 children since she remarried to her second husband.

從她再婚嫁了第二任老公，她一共有 2 個小孩。

duty (noun) 責任

定義 ▶ something you have to do

civic		公民責任
mandatory		強制的責任
family	**duty**	家庭責任
moral		道德責任

實用例句 ·······

out of sense of duty 出於義務
I take care of my sick step-mother out of sense of duty.
出於道義，我照顧我那生病的繼母。

bond (noun) 聯繫 / 相連

定義 a close connection between the two or more people

常用搭配語 ▸ adj + bond

strong		密切聯繫
natural		自然聯繫
emotional	**bond**	情感上的相連
spiritual		精神上的連繫

實用例句 ·······

strong bond of love 愛的互相聯繫
We learn to form a strong bond of love with someone we care.
我們從我們愛的人身上學到愛的互相依附。

🔑 Key Expression
情境表達套用語

comparatively speaking 相對來說
Comparatively speaking, we are more financially better-off.
相對來說，我們算財務狀況較好。

Unit 61

Science & Technology
科學與科技

> Here comes my target!
> 我的目標出現了。

I bought a portable device to track my husband's cell phone.
我買了一個行動型（可攜式）裝置好追蹤我老公的手機。

science (noun) 科學

定義 the system of physical reality

常用搭配語 adj + science

applied		應用科學
exact	science	一門科學
social		社會科學
environmental		環境科學

實用例句 ••••••••••••••••••••••••••••••••••

rocket science 火箭科學（比喻很艱深的事物）
Relax! It is not rocket science.
放鬆！這不會很難的（認真學就會）。

technology (noun) 科技

定義 ► the uses of science

常用搭配語 ► adj + technology

current		現今科技
emerging	**technology**	新興科技
cutting-edge		最新科技
digital		數位科技

◈ 實用例句 ·

Technology is used into daily life.
科技深入生活。

system (noun) 系統

定義 ► a group of related parts that are connected to each other

常用搭配語 ► adj + system

existing		現有的系統
open		公開的系統
foolproof	**system**	萬無一失（連傻瓜都會的）系統
viable		可用 會成功的系統
outdated		過時的系統

◈ 實用例句 ·

existing system 現有系統
We need to replace our existing system, it is running way slow.
我們亟需更換我們的現有系統，它進行的太慢了。

device (noun) 裝置

定義 ► a machine that is designed for a reason.

常用搭配語 ► adj + device

clever		聰明裝置
labor-saving	**device**	節省人力裝置
hand-held		掌上型裝置
warning		警告裝置

實用例句 ••••••••••••••••••••••••••••••

portable device 行動型裝置

I bought a portable device to track my husband's cell phone.

我買了一個行動型（可攜式）裝置好追蹤我老公的手機。

machine (noun) 機器

定義　a piece of equipment with parts that does particular work

常用搭配語　adj + machine

defective		有問題的機器
reliable		可靠的機器
coffee	**machine**	咖啡機
answering		答錄機
vending		販賣機

實用例句 ••••••••••••••••••••••••••••••

complicated machine 複雜的機器

He was sent to Japan to learn how to operate this complicated machine.

他被派到日本去學習如何操作這台複雜的機器。

Key Expression
情境表達套用語

it has just been serviced 才剛維修保養過

Oh!man! This copying machine has just been serviced. And It is acting up now.

喔拜託！這台影印機不是才剛維修保養過。怎麼又再出毛病了。

Senses & Emotion
感官與情感

I really want to have that bag.
我想買那個包包。

She whispered she loved me softly to my ear.
她在我耳邊輕柔地說她愛我。

cry (noun) 哭泣

定義 ▸ to have tears when you feel unhappy or any strong emotions

常用搭配語 ▸ adj + cry

great / loud		大聲哭
hoarse	cry	沙啞的哭泣
agonized		痛苦的哭泣

◈ 實用例句 ••••••••••••••••••••••••••••••••

let out an agonized cry 發出痛苦的哭泣
She let out an agonized cry when the doctor tried to clean her wound.
當醫生在清理她的傷口時，她忍不住發出痛苦的哭泣。

shout (verb) 喊叫

定義 ▸ to say in very loud voice

常用搭配語 ▸ shout + adv

shout	loudly	大吼大叫
	hoarsely	沙啞地喊叫
	angrily	生氣地大叫
	hysterically	歇斯底里地大叫

實用例句 ·····························

shout back 吼回去

Don't shout at me! I will shout back next time!

別對我大吼大叫！我下次就會吼回去！

whisper (verb) 呢喃

定義 ▸ to say with the voice that only someone close to you can hear

常用搭配語 ▸ whisper + adv

whisper	bitterly	痛苦地呢喃
	softly	輕柔地呢喃
	urgently	緊急地在耳邊細語
	back	輕聲回應

實用例句 ·····························

whispered softly 輕柔地呢喃

She whispered she loved me softly to my ear.

她在我耳邊輕柔地說她愛我。

fear (noun) 恐懼

定義 ▸ the feeling that you worry something might happen

常用搭配語 ▸ adj + fear

growing		增長的恐懼
irrational	**fear**	不理性的恐懼
real		真實的恐懼

實用例句 ··

real fear 真正的恐懼

I experienced the real fear from the hijack incident.

從劫機事件中，我經歷過真正的恐懼。

emotion (noun) 情感 / 情緒

定義 all kinds of strong feelings such as love, anger...etc.

常用搭配語 adj + emotion

suppressed		壓抑的情感
inner	**emotion**	內在的情感
positive / negative		正面 / 負面情緒
tangled		糾結的情緒

實用例句 ··

suppressed emotion 壓抑的情緒

When she sobered her heart out, her suppressed emotion came out.

當她大哭一場時，她所有壓抑的情緒都一洩而出。

Key Expression
情境表達套用語

suffer from depression 飽受憂鬱症之苦

My aunt has been suffering from severe depression for many years.

我姑姑已經飽受嚴重憂鬱症之苦好幾年了。

Shopping
購物

I have to run for the last minute.
我快來不及了。

All the shoppers lined up and waited for rushing in and snapping up bargains.
全部的購物狂排好隊等著要衝進去搶購特價好貨。

shopping (noun) 逛街購物

定義 ▶ the activities of buying things from many different shops

常用搭配語 ▶ adj + shopping

home / internet		在家 / 網路購物
weekly		每周一次的購物
duty-free	shopping	免稅購物
one-stop		一站性購物 (全方位)
window		只看不買

🗇 實用例句 ••

do shopping 購物
How often do you do shopping?
你多久購物一次呢？

gift (noun) 禮物

定義 ── the things you bought for someone

常用搭配語 ── adj + gift

expensive		昂貴的禮物
free		免費的禮物
generous		大方的禮物
retirement	gift	退休的禮物
unwanted		不想要的禮物
wedding		結婚的禮物
perfect		完美的禮物
parting		臨別的禮物

◇ 實用例句 ······················

receive gift 收到禮物
We all love to receive gifts, don't we?!
我們大家都愛收到禮物，不是嗎？！

customer (noun) 客戶 / 顧客

定義 ── a shopper who buys goods

常用搭配語 ── adj + customer

key / major		關鍵 / 主要的顧客
current		現有的顧客
regular	customer	老客戶
potential		未來的客戶
unhappy		不開心的顧客
oversea		國外客戶

◇ 實用例句 ······················

lose any customer 流失任何客戶
We can't afford to lose any customer now.
我們現在實在是經不起流失任何客戶了。

cost (noun) 成本

定義 ➤ the amount of money need to spend

常用搭配語 ➤ adj + cost

marginal		邊際成本
star-up		創業成本
estimated		估計成本
extra		多出的成本
average	cost	平均成本
overall		整體成本
rising		上升的成本
low		低成本

📚 實用例句 ....

lower the cost 降低成本
We try our best efforts to lower the cost at this micro project.
我們對這個微專案盡全力要降低成本。

overall cost 整體成本
The overall cost of production is going up.
整體生產成本增加中。

extra cost 多出的成本
The customized specification for this foreign order caused the extra cost.
這張國外下的客製化規格訂單，造成成本多出了。

receipt (noun) 發票

定義 ➤ a piece of paper which proves your purchase

常用搭配語 ➤ verb+ reciept

ask for		要求發票
make out	receipt	開立發票
keep		保留發票

I received my receipt by email.
我用電子郵件收發票。

Always remember to ask for receipt.
要記得索取發票。

Key Expression
情境表達套用語

snap up a bargain 搶購特價品
All the shoppers lined up and waited for rushing in and snapping up bargains.
全部的購物狂排好隊等著要衝進去搶購特價好貨。

Similarity & Difference
相似與差異

> Gorgeous! / Handsome!
> 好美哦！ / 好帥哦！

I do have the different feeling about the movie from hers.
我跟她對那部電影的感覺不同。

similar (adj) 相似的

| 定義 | almost the same |

| 常用搭配語 | adv + similar |

strikingly		驚人地相似
basically	**similar**	基本地相似
roughly		大約地相似
superficially		表面地相似

實用例句

similar in size and capacity 尺寸和容量都很相似
These two items are similar in size and capacity.
這兩個東西尺寸和容量都很相似。

similarity (noun) 相似度

定義 the similar quality in a person or a thing

常用搭配語 verb + similarity

bear / have		有相似度
reveal / show	similarity	展現出相似度
share		共有相似度

實用例句 ···

points of similarity 相似點
She instantly enumerates 3 points of similarity between two products / cases.
她很快地列舉出這兩個產品 / 案子之間三個相似點。

different (adj) 不同的

定義 not the same

常用搭配語 adv + different

radically		根本上地不同
rather	different	相當不同
slightly		稍微不同
subtly		微妙地不同

實用例句 ···

different feeling 感覺不同
I do have the different feeling about the movie from hers.
我跟她對那部電影的感覺不同。

difference (noun) 不同處

定義 the quality that makes one is not the same from the other

常用搭配語 verb + difference

make		有（變）不同處
exaggerate		誇大不同
tell	**difference**	看出不同
examine		分辨不同
reflect		反應出不同點

◈ 實用例句 ·

make any difference 變得不同

I don't think taking his idea will make any difference to our problem.

我不認為用他的方法會讓我們的問題變得不同。

notice (verb) 注意到

定義 ▸ to see or to be aware of something or someone

常用搭配語 ▸ adv + notice

not even		甚至沒注意到
hardly	**notice**	幾乎沒注意到
immediately		立刻注意到
finally		終於注意到

◈ 實用例句 ·

didn't even notice 根本沒注意到

I didn't even notice my boss was standing right behind me.

我壓根兒沒注意到我老闆就站在我後面。

Key Expression
情境表達套用語

it is hard to tell 很難說

Well, it is hard to tell the difference between iphone 6 and iphone 7.

嗯～很難說 iphone 6 和 iphone 7 之間有什麼不同。

Unit 65

Sleep
睡眠

> Somebody help!
> 救命啊！

He jerked awake from a terrible nightmare and cried.
他從一個惡夢中猛然醒過來就哭了。

sleep (noun) 睡眠

定義 ▸ a period of sleep

常用搭配語 ▸ adj + sleep

beauty		美容覺
sound		美好一覺
fitful	**sleep**	斷斷續續的一覺
restless		不得安眠的一覺
dreamless		無夢的一覺

實用例句

I had a good sleep after a long trip.
我長途歸來後睡了一個好覺。

awake (adj) 清醒的

定義 — not sleeping

常用搭配語 — verb + awake

lie		躺著清醒
jerk	**awake**	突然清醒
stay		保持清醒
keep		維持清醒

實用例句 ·····································

jerked awake 猛然醒過來

He jerked awake from a terrible nightmare and cried.

他從一個惡夢中猛然醒過來就哭了。

dream (noun) 夢

定義 — a series of events that happened while you are sleeping

常用搭配語 — adj + dream

awful / bad		噩夢
strange		奇怪的夢
vivid	**dream**	生動鮮明的夢
erotic / wet		有關性愛的夢
prophetic		預言式的夢
undesirable		令人討厭的夢

實用例句 ·····································

I had an undesirable dream last night. I was dumped by my boyfriend in my dream.

我昨晚做了一個很討厭的夢，我夢到我被我男朋友甩了。

nap (noun) 小睡

定義 — short sleep, especially during the day time

常用搭配語 — adj + nap

quick		快速小睡
morning	nap	清晨小睡
afternoon		下午午睡
power		能恢復精力的小睡

實用例句 ·

My energy is back again after taking a 10-minute power nap.
我只要小睡 10 分鐘又會精力充沛了。

room (noun) 房間

定義 ▶ a part of the building that separates others by walls and ceilings

常用搭配語 ▶ adj + room

spacious		寬廣的房間
stuffy		悶熱的房間
windowless	room	無窗戶的房間
quiet		安靜的房間
dingy		髒兮兮的房間
guest / spare		客房 / 空房

實用例句 ·

spare room of my house 我家的空房
I let my visiting friend stay in the spare room of my house.
我讓來拜訪我的朋友住在我家的空房。

Key Expression
情境表達套用語

toss and turn till late night 輾轉難眠到深夜
The coming presentation makes me toss and turn till late night.
即將到的簡報報告讓我輾轉難眠到深夜。

Unit
66

Sounds
聲音

Chime
鐘響聲

All of us can hear the distant sound of the church bell.
我們大家都聽到了來自教堂遠處的聲音。

sound (noun) **聲音**

定義 something you can hear

常用搭配語 adj + sound

distant		遠處的聲音
familiar		熟悉的聲音
strange	sound	奇怪的聲音
buzzing		熱鬧的聲音

實用例句

distant sound 遠處的聲音

All of us can hear the distant sound of the church bell.
我們大家都聽到了來自教堂遠處的聲音。

volume (noun) 音量

定義 ▸ sound level

常用搭配語 ▸ verb + volume

turn up		開大音量
increase	volume	增加音量
turn down		關小音量
decrease		減低音量

實用例句 ·

full / maximum volume 最大音量
I turn up my car stereo at full/maximum volume and move with the beat.
我把車內音響開到最大音量並且隨著節奏擺動。

ear (noun) 耳朵

定義 ▸ body organs for a person or an animal to hear sound

常用搭配語 ▸ adj + ear

right / left		右 / 左耳
torn	ear	撕裂的耳
sympathetic		願意傾聽的耳朵

verb + ear

plug		塞住耳朵
strain	ear	豎起耳朵仔細聽
echo in		耳朵有回音

實用例句 ·

strained my ears to the wall 拉長耳朵貼在牆上（拼命想聽清楚）
I strained my ears to the wall so I can hear what my parents say about my school grades.
我拉長耳朵貼在牆上，這樣我才能聽到我父母對我成績的看法。

hear (verb) 聽到

定義 ▸ to be able to receive the sound by using your ears

常用搭配語 ▸ adv + hear

correctly		正確地聽到
merely	**hear**	幾乎聽不到
distantly		遙遠地聽到
hear	**well**	聽清楚

◈ 實用例句 ·····························

hear well 聽清楚
My dad now is slow and unable to hear well.
我老爸慢吞吞的又聽不清楚。

tune (noun) 曲子 / 旋律

定義 ▸ a melody

常用搭配語 ▸ adj + tune

catchy		容易上口的曲子
theme	**tune**	主題曲
well-known		著名的旋律

◈ 實用例句 ·····························

sing along with a catchy tune 一起哼著一首朗朗上口的曲子
They sing along with a catchy tune on the way back home from work.
他們下班的路上一起哼著一首朗朗上口的曲子回家。

Key Expression
情境表達套用語

let's hear it 說來聽聽 / 洗耳恭聽
Do you have any idea of having fun tonight? Let me hear it!
今晚有什麼玩樂的點子嗎？說來聽聽。

Social

人與人之間

> May friendship live forever!
> 友誼常在！

It takes long time to restore your trust on someone who once betrayed you.
要對一個曾經背叛過你的人重拾信賴感是要花一點時間的。

society (noun) 社會

| 定義 | a large group of people live together in an organized way |

| 常用搭配語 | adj + society |

advanced		進步的社會
traditional		傳統的社會
civilized		文明的社會
affluent	society	富足的社會
democratic		民主的社會
multicultural		多文化的社會
matriarchal		母系社會

build a greater society 讓這個社會更好

Women are now with attention and action to build a greater society.

現代女性有更多精神和行動讓這個社會更好。

development (noun) 發展

| 定義 | the process of growing |

| 常用搭配語 | adj + development |

evolutionary		逐漸進步的發展
educational		教育性的發展
sustainable		永續性的發展
social		社會的發展
rapid	development	快速的發展
economic		經濟的發展
regional		地區的發展
physical		生理的發展
psychological		心裡的發展
property		房地產發展

◈ 實用例句 ･･

technological development 科技發展

There are some drawbacks during our technological development.

在我們的科技發展中仍有一些不好的後果。

trust (noun) 信賴

| 定義 | believe |

| 常用搭配語 | verb + trust |

have		有信賴
put	**trust**	放上信賴（相信）
earn		取得（得到）信賴
restore		重新信賴

實用例句

restore your trust on someone 對一個人重拾信賴感

It takes long time to restore your trust on someone who once betrayed you.

要對一個曾經背叛過你的人重拾信賴感是要花一點時間的。

democracy (noun) 民主

定義 the faith in freedom and equality between people

常用搭配語 adj + democracy

true		真正的民主
multi-party	**democracy**	多黨民主
political		政治性的民主
Western		西方民主

實用例句

true democracy 真正民主

People who fight for true democracy are guardians for this modern society.

為真正民主奮鬥的人是我們現代社會中的守護者。

Western democracy 西方民主

Some of policy was actually borrowed the idea from the Western democracy.

事實上，我們有些政策是從西方民主借鏡而來的。

profile (noun) 印象 / 形象

定義 public image

常用搭配語 verb + profile

give		讓⋯有印象
improve		改善形象
keep	**profile**	保持形象
adopt		選擇或利用形象

 實用例句

keep a low profile 保持低調
She tries to keep a low profile as she is involved in a political scandal.
她試著要保持低調因為她正捲入一場政治醜聞裡。

improve profile 改善形象
She tried to involve in the pro bono to improve her public profile.
她試著從事公益活動，扭轉改善她的大眾形象。

boycott 抵制
Some group of people boycott GM food.
有些人抵制基因改造食物。

Speaking
口說

> I conquered cancer.
> 我戰勝了癌症。

She spoke movingly about how she conquered the cancer.
她動人地訴說她是如何戰勝癌症的。

conversation (noun) 對話

定義 ── a talk involving two people or more

常用搭配語 ── adj + conversation

lengthy		冗長的對話
private	**conversation**	私下的對話
face-to-face		面對面的對話
overheard		無意間聽到的對話

◇ 實用例句 ·

conversation I had with him 我跟他之間的對話

The conversation I had with him was rather uncomfortable.
我跟他之間的對話讓我很不舒服。

speak (verb) 說話

定義 to use your voice to say something

常用搭配語 speak + adv

	boldly	大膽地說
speak	clearly	清楚地說
	movingly	動人地說
	slowly	緩慢地說

實用例句

spoke movingly 動人地訴說
She spoke movingly about how she conquered the cancer.
她動人地訴說她是如何戰勝癌症的。

interrupt (verb) 打斷

定義 to stop a person from talking or something from happening

常用搭配語 adv + interrupt

rudely		沒禮貌地打斷
impatiently		不耐煩地打斷
suddenly	interrupt	突然地打斷
constantly		一直打斷
occasionally		偶爾地打斷

實用例句

Where was I, before I was rudely interrupted？在我剛被沒禮貌地打斷前講到哪了？
How dare you interrupt me！
你好大膽敢插我的話！

explanation (noun) 解釋

定義 the reason you gave to make something easy to understand

常用搭配語 adj + explanation

likely		可能的解釋
reasonable	**explanation**	理性的解釋
implausible		難以置信的解釋
partial		部分的解釋

實用例句

waiting for an explanation 等你一個解釋

I am waiting for an explanation that you owed me.

我在等你欠我的一個解釋。

chant (noun) 說或唱口號

定義 to repeat a word, a phase or a song

常用搭配語 adj + chant

incessant		反覆的說或唱
ballgame	**chant**	球隊口號
melodious		旋律好聽的口號

實用例句

singing the ballgame chant 吟唱著球隊口號

The fans are singing the ballgame chant for the team they support.

球迷們為他們支持的球隊吟唱著球隊口號。

Key Expression
情境表達套用語

have it out with you 跟你攤牌

I am so fed up with you, I am going to have it out with you!

我真的受夠你了！我要和你攤牌說清楚。

Unit 69 | **Self-help**
自助者

Think unthinkable.
勇於逐夢。

Self-awareness is the first step to change yourself.
自我覺醒是改變你自己的第一步。

self-(prefix) **self-** 字首

定義　the quality of a person, such as personality and ability

常用搭配語　self-noun

self-awareness	自我覺醒
self-control	自我控制
self-confidence	自我信心
self-deception	自我欺騙
self-employment	自己經營
self-righteousness	自以為是
self-support	自我支援

 實用例句 ·······························

Self-awareness 自我覺醒

Self-awareness is the first step to change yourself.
自我覺醒是改變你自己的第一步。

promote (verb) 促進 / 推廣

定義 ▸ to encourage sales, development..etc.

常用搭配語 ▸ adv + promote

directly		直接促銷
indirectly		間接促銷
intentionally	promote	故意鼓動
strongly		強力促銷

◈ 實用例句 ·

be strongly promoted 強力促進推廣
The female equal right to work is strongly promoted by a female president.
女性總統強力促進女性的工作平等權。

aid (noun) 援助

定義 ▸ help or support with money or food..etc

常用搭配語 ▸ adj + aid

financial		財務幫助
foreign		國外援助
humanitarian	aid	人道援助
legal		法律援助
medical		醫療援助

◈ 實用例句 ·

relied on foreign aid 仰賴國外援助
Those countries of the third world deeply relied on foreign aid.
第三世界的國家急需仰賴國外援助。

viewpoint (noun) 觀點

定義 ▸ a way of thinking about or looking at things

alternative		另類觀點
contrast	**viewpoint**	相反觀點
narrow		狹隘觀點
personal		個人觀點

實用例句 ···

take alternative viewpoint 從另一角度看
I like to take alternative viewpoint on matters.
我喜歡從另一角度看事情。

respect (noun) 尊敬

定義　to show admiration to someone or something

常用搭配語　adj + respect

deep		深深的尊敬
grudging	**respect**	不由得尊敬
mutual		相互的尊敬

實用例句 ···

grudging respect 不得不尊敬
She finally won the grudging respect of the whole team.
她終於讓整個團隊不得不尊敬她。

Key Expression
情境表達套用語

live up to someone's expectation 沒達到某人的期望
I feel sorry that I didn't live up to my parent's expectation.
我對我沒達到父母親的期望感到很抱歉。

Sports & Recreation
運動與娛樂

> I want to be slim.
> 我要成為瘦子。

I had better take up a sport to shed off some weight.
我最好做運動來減重。

sport (noun) 運動

定義 ➤ physical activities for competition or purely enjoyment

常用搭配語 ➤ adj + sport

popular		流行的運動
contact		肢體接觸的運動
grueling		筋疲力盡的運動
risky		危險的運動
outdoor	sport	戶外的運動
indoor		室內的運動
individual		個人的運動
team		團體的運動
amateur		業餘的運動
professional		專業的運動

take up a sport 作（從事）運動

I had better take up a sport to shed off some weight.

我最好作運動來減重。

recreation (noun) 休閒活動

定義 ▸ the activities you enjoy when you are not working

常用搭配語 ▸ adj + recreation

popular		大眾休閒
main	recreation	主要休閒
countryside		鄉野休閒
indoor		室內休閒

實用例句 ⬦ •

form of recreation 休閒型態

What is your form of recreation when you stay home?

你在家時都從事什麼休閒呢？

player (noun) 球員 / 玩家

定義 ▸ someone who play in a game or sport

常用搭配語 ▸ adj + player

talented		有天分的運動員
top	player	頂尖的運動員
average		普通的球員
professional		專業的球員

實用例句 ⬦ •

professional players 專業球員

This suit is for professional players rather than for average ones.

這球衣是給專業球員穿的而不是一般的球員。

team (noun) 隊伍球隊

定義　　　a group of people play a game or sport

常用搭配語　　　verb + team

put together		組成隊伍
coach		教導隊伍
play for		為球隊比賽
be selected for	team	被選為球隊
be dropped from		被踢出球隊
make		加入球隊
lead		領導球隊

◈ 實用例句 ....

make the team 加入球隊
I am sorry to hear that you didn't make the team.
我很抱歉你無法加入球隊。

lead the whole team 獨當一面
After the 5 years of honing skills, he is finally able to lead the whole team.
經過 5 年的磨練技巧，他終於能獨當一面了。

training (noun) 訓練

定義　　　a process of learning skills

常用搭配語　　　adj + training

initial		初次訓練
extensive		加強訓練
intensive		密集訓練
proper		正確訓練
hands-on	training	由做中學的訓練
vocational		職業訓練
work-related		工作相關的訓練
physical		體能訓練

vocational training 職業訓練
This job will require you to undergo a year-long vocational training.
這個工作將需要你進行為期一年的職業訓練。

intensive training 密集的訓練
I have been put through the intensive training to become a good teacher.
我要接受密集的訓練才能成為一位好老師。

Key Expression
情境表達套用語

sporty thermal hoodie 發熱運動用連帽外套
We definitely need the sporty thermal hoodie to fight back the freezing winter.
這個寒冬我們不能沒有會發熱的運動用連帽外套。

Success
成功

I can make it.
我會成功的！

I must say that your input is essential to success of this project.
我必須說你的投入對這個專案的成功是必要的。

win (noun) 勝利

定義　an act of achieving first place or getting a prize in a game or contest

常用搭配語　adj + win

easy		易如反掌的獲勝
decisive		決定性的勝利
impressive		印象深刻的勝利
narrow	win	險勝
impressive		令人印象深刻的勝利
deserved		應得的勝利
unexpected		意想不到的勝利
handsome		贏的漂亮

impressive win 令人印象深刻的比賽

People are still talking about baseball team's impressive win against Japan.

人們到現在還津津樂道那場令人印象深刻對戰日本的棒球比賽。

easy win 易如反掌

It was an easy win for the professional against amateur.

職業的對上業餘的比賽，簡直是易如反掌的獲勝。

success (noun) 成功

| 定義 | something worked out and won money, respect or fame |

| 常用搭配語 | verb + success |

be vital to		對成功極為重要
bring		帶來成功
guarantee	**success**	保證成功
achieve / enjoy		獲得 / 享受成功
lead to		導向成功

◇ 實用例句 ••

be essential to success 對成功是必要的

I must say that your input is essential to success of this project.

我必須說你的投入對這個專案的成功是必要的。

guarantee success 保證成功

It's now common sense that hard work always guarantees success.

努力工作總是能保證成功，這是再正常不過的事了。

result (noun) 結果

| 定義 | outcome or conclusion |

| 常用搭配語 | verb + result |

get		得到結果
give		得到結果
have / produce	result	產生結果
come up with		產生結果
show		出現結果

🗇 實用例句 ···

hard work shows no result 努力工作一無所獲的結果
I feel miserable that my hard work shows no result.
我對於我努力工作一無所獲的結果感到很悲哀。

deserve (verb) 該得 / 得到

定義 ▸ you earned something for what you did

常用搭配語 ▸ adv + deserve

certainly		當然該得
truly	deserve	真的該得
fully		完全應得
hardly		不該得到

🗇 實用例句 ···

hardly deserve 也不該
She might make some tiny mistakes but she hardly deserves to be fired.
她或許有犯一些小錯誤，但她也不該被解雇。

certainly deserved 理應得到
The way she devoted herself to the company, she certainly deserved a raise.
她為公司那麼盡心盡力，她理應得到加薪。

progress (noun) 進步

定義 ▸ to keep going on improving

facilitate		促進進步
make		增加進步
monitor	**progress**	檢視進步
track		追蹤進步
slow down		讓進度放慢

實用例句

progress report 進度表

Geeeez, I guess I have to stay up charting my progress report that is due on Monday.

天阿，我看我得熬夜製作下星期一要交的進度表了。

track the progress 追蹤進度

The manager stands behind us to track the progress of preparation for the report.

經理站在後面追蹤我們準備報告的進度。

Key Expression
情境表達套用語

pass with flying colors 高分過關

I am crossing my fingers that I will pass with flying colors on the exam.

我正在祈禱我考試高分過關。

Unit 72

Tastes & Smells
味道和氣味

> Coffee smells so good !
> 咖啡好香哦！

This coffee shop is always filled with the rich aroma of coffee.
這間咖啡店總是瀰漫著濃厚咖啡香味。

taste (noun) 口味 / 味道

定義	flavor

常用搭配語 ▸ adj + taste

delicious		美味的味道
strong		強烈的味道
mild		溫和的味道
nasty	taste	噁心的味道
salty		鹹味
spicy		辣味
authentic		招牌的味道

◈ 實用例句 ·······················

have a taste 嚐嚐看味道

Hon, have a taste of the cake I made for our anniversary.
親愛的，嚐嚐看我為我們周年紀念日特別作的蛋糕。

smell (noun) 氣味

| 定義 | the ability to smell odor or aroma |

| 常用搭配語 | adj + smell |

lovely		美妙的氣味
overpowering		讓人受不了的氣味
funny		奇怪的氣味
awful	smell	糟糕的氣味
stale		發霉的氣味
cooking		煮食物的味道
fishy		魚腥味

◇ 實用例句 ••

funny smell 怪味道
Ew~ What's the funny smell in your bedroom?
噁～你房間那是什麼怪味道？

aroma (noun) 香味

| 定義 | a pleasant smell |

| 常用搭配語 | adj + aroma |

strong		強烈的香味
lingering	aroma	持續的香味
wonderful		美好的香味
mouth-watering		令人流口水的香味

◇ 實用例句 ••

rich aroma of coffee 濃厚咖啡香味
This coffee shop is always filled with the rich aroma of coffee.
這間咖啡店總是瀰漫著濃厚咖啡香味。

mouth-watering aroma 令人流口水的香味

There is always a mouth-watering aroma in that bakery.

那家麵包店總是散發著令人流口水的香味。

odor (noun) 臭味

定義 ▸ a smell, is often the unpleasant one

常用搭配語 ▸ adj + odor

body		體臭味
stale		發霉臭味
obnoxious		令人討厭的臭味
pungent		刺鼻的臭味
faint	odor	輕微的臭味
unmistakable		明顯的臭味
foul		臭死人了
familiar		熟悉的臭味

實用例句

awful body odor 惱人的體臭

I usually use deodorant to get rid of my awful body odor.

我通常會用體香劑來消除我那惱人的體臭。

pungent odor 刺鼻的臭味

Lots of foreigners hate the pungent odor from stinky tofu.

很多外國人都痛恨臭豆腐那刺鼻的臭味。

flavor (noun) 口味

定義 ▸ the taste of food or drink

常用搭配語 ▸ adj + flavor

exotic		異國風味
extra		加重口味
nutty		堅果口味
smoky	flavor	煙燻口味
mellow		成熟的口味
unique		獨特的口味

實用例句

minty flavor 清涼薄荷味
This soda drink has got a minty flavor.
這個蘇打汽水帶有清涼薄荷味。

unique flavor 口味獨特
That pizza store is famous for making unique flavor for customers.
那家比薩店以製作口味獨特的比薩聞名。

Key Expression
情境表達套用語

a whiff of garlic 一股大蒜的味道
I caught a whiff of garlic when he talked in my face.
當他當著我的面說話時，我聞到一陣大蒜的味道。

Unit
73

Technology & Gadget
科技與產品

Big data era has come.
Bit data 大數據時代來臨。

I will soon share all my data analysis on cloud.
我很快地會在雲端分享我所有的數據分析資料。

phone (noun) 電話

定義 a hand-held device for someone to contact people

常用搭配語 verb + phone

answer		回答電話
pick up		接電話
hang up		掛上電話
smash	phone	摔電話
bug		竊聽電話
wait by		守在電話旁

🗇 實用例句 ··

on the phone 講電話

She is on the phone talking to her friend / broker.
她正在跟她的朋友 / 經紀人講電話。

message (noun) 訊息

a short piece of information that you give someone

verb + message

pass on		傳遞訊息
text	**message**	打簡訊
leave		留訊息
get		得到訊息

實用例句

texted my mom a message 傳簡訊給我媽
I just texted my mom a message not to wait up for me.
我剛才傳簡訊給我媽叫她不要等我的門。

gadget (noun) 小裝置 / 器具

a small device

adj + gadget

electronic		電子裝置
kitchen		廚房器具
latest	**gadget**	最新工具
neat		很棒的工具
useless		沒用的裝置

實用例句

the latest handy gadget 最新實用小玩意兒
Helen, come and check out the latest handy gadget I bought for slicing apples.
Helen，快來看看我剛買的切蘋果的最新實用小玩意兒。

There are hundreds of electronic gadgets to choose from for improving our life.
有上百種的電子裝置可選擇用來改善我們的生活。

target (noun) 目標

定義 ► something that you aim to reach

常用搭配語 ► verb + target

aim for		針對目標
set		設定目標
meet		達到目標
stay with	**target**	持續目標
exceed		超出目標
fall short of		未達到目標

◈ 實用例句 ··

exceed the sales target 超出營業目標

My boss expects me to exceed the sales target this month.

我老闆期待我這個月要超出營業目標。

set a target of 設定目標

I've decided to set a target of saving 5,000 per month.

我決定要設定每個月存 5000 元的目標。

data (noun) 資料數據

定義 ► information or a set of numbers collected to be examined or used for decision making

常用搭配語 ► verb + data

collect		收集資料
enter		輸入資料
store		儲存資料
retrieve	**data**	檢索資料
analyze		分析資料
process		處理資料
transfer		轉存資料

data analysis 數據分析資料

I will soon share all my data analysis on cloud.

我很快地會在雲端分享我所有的數據分析資料。

collect data 收集資料

The cyber criminals steal and collect personal data from internet users.

網路犯罪者從網路用戶上竊取並收集個人資料。

Key Expression
情境表達套用語

make a phone call 打一通電話

Excuse me, I really need to make a phone call now.

不好意思，我現在必須打一通電話。

Unit 74

Test
考試

English is not Greek to me anymore!
英文對我來說不再難懂了！

After burying my nose in English for half a year, I finally did improve my TOEFL.
在埋頭苦讀英文半年後，我的托福考試終於有進步了。

study (noun) 研究

定義 ▶ a piece of research

常用搭配語 ▶ adj + study

recent		最近的研究
earlier		先前的研究
empirical		臨床研究
feasibility		可行性研究
case		案例研究
pilot	study	初步研究
comparative		差異性研究
scientific		科學研究
sociological		社會研究
close		仔細研究

the recent study shows 最近的研究顯示

The recent study shows the link between obesity and socioeconomic status.

最近的研究顯示肥胖症和社會經濟地位之間的相關性。

improve (verb) 改善

定義 ▶ to make something better

常用搭配語 ▶ adv + improve

dramatically		驚人地改善
noticeably		明顯地改善
slightly	**improve**	稍微地改善
rapidly		快速地改善
steadily		穩定地改善

⬦ **實用例句** ‧‧‧‧‧‧‧‧‧‧‧‧‧‧‧‧‧‧‧‧‧‧‧‧‧‧‧‧‧‧‧‧‧‧‧‧‧‧

improve my TOEFL 改善托福考試

After burying my nose in English for half a year, I finally did improve my TOEFL.

在我埋頭苦讀英文半年後，我的托福考試終於有變好了。

noticebly improved 明顯地進步

His math noticebly improved by studying with a tutor.

靠著跟家教一起念，他的數學明顯地進步了。

review (verb) 複習

定義 ▶ go over what you have studied

常用搭配語 ▶ adv + review

briefly		簡短地複習
from time to time	**review**	有時偶爾的複習
fully		完整的複習
regularly		經常的複習

regularly review 經常會複習
I regularly review the notes I made during the class.
我經常會複習我在課堂上作的筆記。

theme (noun) 主題

定義　the main subject

常用搭配語　adj + theme

broad		寬廣的主題
common		普通的主題
familiar		熟悉的主題
key	theme	關鍵性的主題
related		相關的主題
research		研究主題

◈ 實用例句 ···

give a talk on the theme of 發表一個主題演說
I was told to give a talk on the theme of juvenile delinquency.
我受邀發表一個主題關於青少年犯罪的演說。

course (noun) 課程

定義　a set of classes or a plan of study

常用搭配語　adj + course

all-day		全日課程
two-year		二年的課程
crash		快速課程
advanced	course	進階課程
introductory		入門課程
refresher		進修課程

sandwich	course	工讀交替課程
training		訓練課程
undergraduate		大學課程

📚 實用例句 ···

crash course in Japanese 日文的快速課程
I have decided to take a crash course in Japanese.
我決定要去上日文的快速課程。

two-year course 唸二年的課程
I think I am lucky to be able to take two-year course on scholarship.
我想我很幸運的能夠靠獎學金唸二年的課程。

Key Expression
情境表達套用語

have something to do with 跟⋯⋯有關
I just can't get it why Physics has something to do with my future job.
我就是搞不懂為什麼物理會跟我未來的工作有關。

Unit 75 | Time & Space
時間與空間

I really hate standing in line.
我討厭排隊。

I am so sick and tired of taking ages to check out in a long line.
我對耗時間大排長龍等結帳真的很厭惡。

time (noun) 時間

定義 ▶ the existence that is measured in seconds, minutes, hours, days or years

常用搭配語 ▶ time + verb

	goes by	時間過去
time	fly	時間飛逝
	drag	時間拖延
	heal	時間療癒

實用例句 ·····························

time can heal my pain 時間可以治療我的痛苦
Only time can heal my pain of being cheated.
只有時間可以治療我被欺騙的痛苦。

space (noun) 空間

定義 ➤ an empty area

常用搭配語 ➤ verb + space

make use of		善用空間
take up		占用空間
create	space	創造空間
waste		浪費空間
save		節省空間
stare into		凝視虛空

📑 實用例句 ···

takes too much space 占了太多空間了
My piano takes too much space in the living room.
我的鋼琴占了客廳太多空間了。

stare into space 凝視虛空
The class I went taught me how to meditate and stare into space.
我去上的課，教我如何冥想並凝視虛空。

span (noun) 持續時間

定義 ➤ the length of time

常用搭配語 ➤ adj + span

long		長時間
1-week	span	一周的時間
allotted		分配的時間
attention		注意力時間

📑 實用例句 ···

short attention span 注意力時間短暫
Joe has a short attention span for things uninteresting.
Joe 對不感興趣的事物注意力時間很短。

plan (noun) 計畫

定義 ▸ a thought of doing things in the future

常用搭配語 ▸ verb + plan

come up with		提出計畫
cancel		取消計畫
discuss		討論計畫
launch	plan	開始計畫
implement		執行計畫
stick to		堅持計畫

📚 實用例句 ••

came up with a plan 想到一個計畫
Hey, I came up with a plan to double my income.
欸，我想到一個可以讓我收入加倍的計畫耶！

stick to plan 堅持計畫
No matter what happened, we must stick to our plan.
無論發生任何事，我們都務必堅持計畫。

gap (noun) 代溝 / 間隔

定義 ▸ difference

常用搭配語 ▸ adj + gap

age		年齡代溝
culture		文化代溝
credibility		信用差距（指保證之事與實際情況間的差異）
gender	gap	性別代溝
growing		增加的間隔
knowledge		知識代溝
huge		鴻溝

politician's creditability gap 政客說一套做一套的行為
I am really fed up with some politician's creditability gap.
我真的受夠了有些政客說一套做一套的風格行為。

culture gap 文化代溝
The culture gap in Taiwan has been growing increasingly at an alarming rate.
台灣的文化差異代溝，正以驚人的速度增加中。

Key Expression
情境表達套用語

take ages 耗費大量時間
I am so sick and tired of taking ages to check out in a long line.
我對耗時間大排長龍等結帳真的很厭惡。

Unit 76

Travel
旅行

> Hoooray! I've saved up enough money.
> 我錢存夠了。

Sooner or later I will save up enough money and travel around the world.
我遲早會存夠錢環遊世界。

travel (verb) 旅行

定義 ▸ to make a journey

常用搭配語 ▸ travel + adv

travel	abroad	出國旅行
	back and forth	來回旅行
	business class	坐商務艙旅行
	independently	自由行
	together	一起旅行
	regularly	經常旅行

◈ **實用例句** ··································

travel business class 坐商務艙旅行
I used to travel business class before losing my job.
我還沒丟掉工作前都坐商務艙旅行。

nation (noun) 國家

定義 ▸ a country

常用搭配語 ▸ adj + nation

affluent		富裕的國家
backward		落後的國家
civilized		文明的國家
industrialized	**nation**	工業化的國家
emerging		新興的國家
oil-producing		產油的國家
powerful		強國

實用例句 ··

democratic nation 民主的國家

Taiwan is a compact and democratic nation.

台灣是一個精密和民主的國家。

custom (noun) 風土 / 民俗

定義 ▸ what the local people believe and act for long time

常用搭配語 ▸ verb + custom

follow		追隨風俗
observe		觀察民俗
respect	**custom**	尊重風俗
preserve		保存民俗
revive		活化民俗

adj + custom

ancient		古代風俗
traditional		傳統民俗
local	**custom**	當地風俗
social		社會風俗
quaint		奇怪的風俗

custom between nations 各國風俗
Custom between nations varies.
各國風俗都不一樣。

preserve and revive custom 保存和活化風俗
The aboriginal tried hard to preserve and revive their own custom.
原住民努力嘗試保存和活化他們自己的風俗。

sight (noun) 景點

定義 ▸ places in your travel

常用搭配語 ▸ adj + sight

famous		著名景點
historic	sight	歷史景點

verb + sight

see		觀賞景點
visit	sight	參觀景點

實用例句 ∙∙

visiting the different sights of 探訪多個不同景點
We are all exhausted after visiting the different sights of Taipei in one day.
在一天內探訪這麼多個台北景點我們都累翻了。

traffic (noun) 交通

定義 ▸ the condition of vehicles moving along roads

常用搭配語 ▸ adj + traffic

bad		交通壅擠
light		車流不多的交通
slow-moving		行車緩慢的交通
air	**traffic**	航空交通
local		當地交通
rush-hour		上下班交通高峰車流

實用例句

horrible traffic jam 可怕的塞車
I have stuck in this horrible traffic jam for almost an hour.
我已經陷在這個可怕的塞車陣中快一小時了。

I 'm sorry that I will be slightly late as traffic is the murder.
我很抱歉我會稍微地遲到，因為交通害的。

Key Expression
情境表達套用語

sooner or later 遲早
Sooner or later I will save up enough money and travel around the world.
我遲早會存夠錢環遊世界。

Unit 77

Truth & Lies
真實與謊言

> I have a confession to make.
> 我想坦白說一件事。

I can't hide it anymore. I have a confession to make.
我不能再躲避了，我有一件事要坦白。

truth (noun) 事實 / 真相

定義 ▶ the fact that is true

常用搭配語 ▶ verb + truth

accept		接受事實
admit		承認事實
face	truth	面對事實
doubt		懷疑事實
know		知道事實
tell		告訴真相

實用例句 ·······························

know the truth 知道事實
Now you know the truth. What are you going to do?
現在真相大白了，你打算怎麼辦？

lie (noun) 謊言

定義 say something which is not true

常用搭配語 ▶ adj + lie

big		漫天大謊
little		輕微小謊
white	lie	善意的謊言
obvious		明顯的謊言

實用例句 ·

machine of making lies 說謊的機器
Don't take his word for it. He is a machine of making lies.
千萬別相信他說的話,他是個說謊的機器。

white lie 善意的謊言
Telling a white lie sometimes is an art.
說善意的謊言有時是一門藝術。

honest (adj) 誠實

定義 ▶ to be able to tell a truth

常用搭配語 ▶ adv + honest

absolutely		絕對地誠實
basically		基本上地誠實
truly	honest	真正地誠實
not entirely		不是全部地誠實
painfully		痛苦地誠實

實用例句 ·

brutally honest 殘酷地誠實
Let us be brutally honest. I do think this job won't get you anywhere!
讓我們殘酷地誠實一點,我不覺得你做這工作會有出息!

fact (noun) 事實

定義 something that truly happens

常用搭配語 verb + fact

be aware of		留意事實
be based on		以事實為主
hide		隱藏事實
ignore	fact	忽略事實
deny		否認事實
prove		證明事實
find out		發現事實

◈ 實用例句

fact is often ignored 事實經常被忽略
This fact is often ignored by people.
這個事實經常被人們忽略。

find out the fact 找出真相
I'll try everything to find out the fact.
我會盡全力找出真相。

confession (noun) 告白

定義 when someone admitted that he/she has done something wrong

常用搭配語 verb + confession

make		告白
extract	confession	設法得到告白
retract		收回告白

◈ 實用例句

confession to make 公開坦白

I can't hide it anymore. I have a confession to make.
我不能再躲避了，我有一件事要坦白。

made a confession 告解
He went to the church and made a confession to the father.
他去了教堂並向神父告解。

Key Expression
情境表達套用語

use deception to 利用欺騙手法
Shopping Channels sometimes used deception to make the false image of how perfect the product is.
購物頻道有時會利用欺騙手法製造產品非常完美的假象。

Unit 78

Vacation & Destination
假期和目的地

Happy time!
快樂時光！

Yay, my boss is going on family vacation. When the cat's away, the mice will play!
耶！我老闆全家去渡假了，貓不在，老鼠可以作怪了！

area (noun) 地區

定義 ▸ a part of place, a piece of land

常用搭配語 ▸ adj + area

conservation		保護區
coastal		海岸區
deprived		貧窮區
local	area	當地地區
surrounding		四周地區
residential		住宅區
urban		都會區
rural		鄉野地區

coastal area 海岸區
I grew up here and I know the coastal area very well.
我在這裡長大而且我很了解這裡的海岸區。

deprived area 貧窮區
Normally, people don't set their foot in deprived area of the city.
正常來說，大家通常不會踏入城市中的貧窮區。

suburb (noun) 郊區

| 定義 | the outer area of a city |

| 常用搭配語 | adj + suburb |

wealthy		有錢人住的郊區
quiet	**suburb**	安靜的郊區
pleasant		宜人的郊區
sprawling		無規畫延伸的郊區

⬨ 實用例句 ●●●

move in the suburbs 搬到郊區去
We have decided to move in the suburbs, the rent is way much cheaper than that of city.
我們決定要搬到郊區，因為房租比城市便宜太多了。

quiet suburb 安靜郊區
The reason why I moved to a quiet suburb is to recuperate from my chronic pain.
我搬到安靜郊區的原因，是調養我的長年病痛。

vision (noun) 景象

| 定義 | the sight you see |

horrible		糟糕的景象
bleak	vision	荒涼的景象
mysterious		神秘的景象
poetic		充滿詩意的景象

◇ 實用例句 ···

Standing in the canyon, I experienced the magnificent yet bleak vision.
站在大峽谷裡，我感受到了巨大又荒涼的景象。

glance (noun) 一眼

定義 ▶ to give a quick short look at something

常用搭配語 ▶ adj + glance

angry		生氣的一眼
mocking		嘲笑的一眼
casual	glance	隨興的一眼
curious		好奇的一眼
sidelong		斜看一眼

◇ 實用例句 ···

gave me a sidelong glance 斜著眼睛看了我一眼
My boss gave me a sidelong glance and walked away.
我老闆斜著眼睛看了我一眼就走開了。

destination (noun) 目的地

定義 ▶ the place at which you plan to arrive

常用搭配語 ▶ adj + destination

final		最終目的地
ideal	**destination**	理想的目的地
exotic		異國渡假地
holiday		渡假勝地

實用例句

perfect destination 完美渡假地

Koh Samui is a perfect destination for honey moon goers.

蘇美島真是一個度蜜月者的完美度假地。

exotic destination 異國情調

I'm really looking forward to a vacation in an exotic destination.

我好期待在一個異國情調的地方渡假。

Key Expression
情境表達套用語

go on vacation 去渡假

Yay, my boss is going on family vacation. When the cat's away, the mice will play!

耶！我老闆全家去渡假了，貓不在，老鼠可以作怪了！

Unit 79 | **Weather**
天氣

Hey, I'm ready to attack now!
嘿嘿！我準備要發威了。

The horrible storm lasted for 3 days.
這可怕的暴風雨持續了 3 天。

學會別人不會的特殊計量詞 !!!

a clap of	thunder	一聲雷響
a bolt of	lightning	一道閃電
a drift of	snow	一堆積雪
a drop of	rain	一滴雨 / 一陣下雨
a gust of	wind	一陣風
a ray of	sunlight	一縷陽光

storm (noun) 風暴

定義 ▶ a bad weather situation with heavy rain, strong wind, thunder and lightning

常用搭配語 ▶ storm + verb

storm	hit something	風暴襲擊
	be coming	風暴即將來臨
	subside	風暴趨緩
	last	風暴持續

實用例句

horrible storm lasted 可怕的暴風雨持續
The horrible storm lasted for 3 days.
這可怕的暴風雨持續了 3 天。

storm is coming 即將來臨
The sky is so dark right now, I think the storm is coming.
天空變的烏黑，我看暴風雨即將來臨。

winter (noun) 冬季

定義 ▶ the coldest season of a year

常用搭配語 ▶ winter + noun

winter	clothes	冬季衣物
	sports	冬季運動
	solstice	冬至
	break	寒假
	scene	冬季景致
	weather	冬季天氣

實用例句

Winter solstice makes the shortest day and the longest night of the year.
冬至造成了一年之中最短的白天和最長的夜晚。

winter break 寒假
Every child is looking forward to the winter break.
每一個小孩都在滿心期待寒假的到來。

rain (noun) 雨

定義 ▸ drops of water from clouds

常用搭配語 ▸ adj + rain

constant		持續下雨
pouring		傾盆大雨
intermittent	**rain**	時下時停的雨
tropical		熱帶雨

◈ 實用例句 ·······································

monsoon rain 雨季的雨

Some countries will pray for monsoon rain for their harvests.

有些國家會為了收成祈求雨季的雨快來。

Key Expression
情境表達套用語

Weather is fickle. 天氣多變化。

Weather is fickle, and so are you!

天氣善變，而你也一樣！。

World view
世界觀

> Sit up tall while you're seated.
> 坐的時候要抬頭挺胸

GOOD

Manners

We are taught to behave properly in front of elders.
我們被教導在長輩面前要表現得體。

behave (verb) 行為 / 表現

| 定義 | to act in certain way |

| 常用搭配語 | behave + adv |

	well	表現良好
	badly	表現差
behave	properly	表現得體
	oddly	表現怪異
	naturally	表現自然

實用例句

behave **properly** 表現得體

We are taught to behave properly in front of elders.
我們被教導在長輩面前要表現得體。

widespread (adj) 廣泛的

> **定義** ▸ happened in many places

> **常用搭配語** ▸ adv + widespread

extremely		極度地廣泛
increasingly	**widespread**	越來越廣泛
sufficiently		非常地廣泛
geographically		遍布地區

◈ 實用例句 ··

geographically widespread 地理遍佈廣泛

English is a geographically widespread language.

英語是一個地理遍佈廣泛的語言。

controversy (noun) 爭議

> **定義** ▸ a lot of arguments about something

> **常用搭配語** ▸ adj + controversy

fierce		激烈的爭議
major		主要的爭議
continuing		不斷的爭議
public		公眾的爭議
religious	**controversy**	宗教的爭議
considerable		相當大 / 多的爭議
renewed		重新燃起的爭議
raging		令人憤怒的爭議
academic		學術上的爭議

◈ 實用例句 ··

major network controversy 主要網際網路的爭議

Facebook has run into a major network controversy about user's privacy.

有關臉書使用者的隱私權，已經造成了主要網際網路的爭議。

continuing controversy 不斷爭論的議題

Abortion has been the continuing controversy between the religionists and atheists for decades.

墮胎數十年來一直是宗教者和無神論者不斷爭論的議題。

world (noun) 世界

定義 the Earth

常用搭配語 world + noun

world	economy	世界經濟
	recession	世界不景氣
	champion	世界冠軍
	record	世界紀錄
	tour	世界巡迴演出
	ranking	世界排名
	class	世界級

實用例句

embarking on world tour 開始世界巡迴演出

My favorite band is close to embarking on world tour.

我最愛的樂團即將要開始世界巡迴演出了。

world recession 全世界不景氣

Due to the world recession,people have held off on buying new cars and taking vacation overseas.

由於全世界不景氣的關係,大家都延緩買新車和海外渡假。

peace (noun) 和平

定義 to be free from war and violence

常用搭配語 peace + noun

peace	envoy	和平大使
	conference	和平會議
	talks	和平會談
	agreement	和平協議
	movement	和平行動

實用例句

peace envoy 和平大使
She was appointed as a peace envoy to the third world country.
她被任命為前往第三世界國家的和平大使。

Key Expression
情境表達套用語

face strong competition 面臨強大競爭
Due to the globalization, many companies are now facing the strong competition.
由於全球化,許多家公司現正面臨強大競爭。

Work experience & Places
工作經驗與環境

I'm working overseas.
我要去海外工作了。

Only one lucky applicant will earn the chance to work and play overseas.
只有一位幸運的求職者能獲得海外度假打工的機會。

career (noun) 事業 / 行業

定義	the job that you do for a long time

常用搭配語	adj + career

professional		專業的事業 / 行業
successful		成功的事業 / 行業
teaching	**career**	教書的事業 / 行業
promising		有前途的事業 / 行業
flagging		沒落的事業 / 行業

實用例句 ·····················

flagging career 搖搖欲墜的事業
I really need a boost for my flagging career.
我真的需要給我那搖搖欲墜的事業加一把勁。

applicant (noun) 求職者 / 申請者

定義 ▶ a person who is applying for a job or admission of a school

常用搭配語 ▶ adj + applicant

lucky		幸運的求職者
potential	**applicant**	有潛力的求職者
suitable		合適的求職者
disappointed		失望的求職者

🗇 實用例句

lucky applicant 幸運的求職者
Only one lucky applicant will earn the chance to work and play overseas.
只有一位幸運的求職者能獲得海外度假打工的機會。

qualification (noun) 資格 / 條件

定義 ▶ a formal record showing that you have skill/knowledge for a job

常用搭配語 ▶ adj + qualification

minimum		最低資格
necessary		必須條件
management	**qualification**	管理資格證明
educational		教育資格證書
technical		技術資格證明

🗇 實用例句

minimum qualification 最低條件
The minimum qualification for this job is master degree.
這工作的條件至少要碩士畢業。

workload (noun) 工作量

定義 ▸ the amount of work to be done

常用搭配語 ▸ adj + workload

heavy		工作量大
excessive		過多工作量
increased	**workload**	增加的工作量
reduced		減少的工作量
administrative		行政管理工作量

◈ 實用例句 ··

heavy workload 繁重的工作量
I do need an assistant to ease my heavy workload.
我真的需要一位助理來減輕我繁重的工作量。

increased workload 日漸增加的工作量
I desperately need some better ways to manage my increased workload.
我超級需要一些好的方法，來處理我日漸增加的工作量。

pay (noun) 薪水

定義 ▸ the money you get for the work you have done

常用搭配語 ▸ adj + pay

monthly / weekly		月 / 週薪
full / half		全 / 半薪
high / low		高 / 低薪
maternity	**pay**	生產薪資
holiday		假日薪
overtime		加班薪
severance		遣散費

實用例句

equal pay 薪資平等
We should have demanded the equal pay between men and women.
我們早該要求男女薪資要平等。

holiday pay 假日薪
Employers should know the intangible value of holiday pay and it improves the overall morale,too.
雇主應該知道假日薪的無形價值,而且它還能全面提升員工士氣。

Key Expression
情境表達套用語

Someone likes to wheel everything. 某人愛指使所有的事。
My boss really likes to wheel everything!
我老闆真的很愛頤指氣使所有的事!

Unit 82

Writing
寫作

It's a dream come true.
夢想成真！

I dream about becoming a female travel writer one day.
我夢想有一天要成為女性旅遊作家。

writing (noun) 寫作

定義 to put your thought into words

常用搭配語 adj + writing

creative		創意寫作
effective	writing	有效的寫作
technical		科技寫作
travel		旅遊寫作

實用例句 ···

creative writing 創意寫作
I recently took a creative writing course.
我最近去上了創意寫作的課程。

writer (noun) 作家

定義 ► a person who writes articles or books

常用搭配語 ► adj + writer

aspiring		鼓舞人心的作家
award-winning		獲獎的作家
best-selling		暢銷書作家
freelance	writer	自由作家
influential		有影響力的作家
prolific		作品豐富的作家
ghost		幫人代筆的作家

實用例句

female travel writer 女性旅遊作家
I dream about becoming a female travel writer one day.
我夢想有一天要成為女性旅遊作家。

award winning writer 獲獎無數的作家
Christopher Hitchens is terribly missed, was an award winning writer, critic and journalist.
我們非常懷念克里多夫希欽斯，一個獲獎無數的作家、評論家和記者。

influentail writers 有影響力的作家
Ayn Rand was one of the most influential writers in novel and philosophy.
艾茵蘭德是小說和哲學界中，最具有影響力的作家之一。

novel (noun) 小說

定義 ► a long-written story about imaginary people and events

常用搭配語 ► adj + novel

acclaimed	novel	受到讚賞的小說
paperback		平裝本小說

latest		最新出版的小說
modern	**novel**	現代小說
adventure		冒險小說

實用例句 ·

a copy of romantic novel 一本浪漫小說

I grabbed a copy of romantic novel with me before I left home.

我離家前拿了一本浪漫小說在身上。

book (noun) 書

定義 　a long-written work that can be read

常用搭配語 　adj + book

forthcoming		即將出版的書
second-hand		二手書
useful	**book**	有用的書
controversial		具爭議性的書
reference		參考書

實用例句 ·

second-hand book price 二手書的價錢

I am going to sell some of my books with second-hand book price.

我要把一些我的書用二手書的價錢賣掉。

forthcoming book 即將出版的新書

Everyone is on the edge of the seat to her forthcoming book.

大家都專注在她即將出版的新書。

reader (noun) 讀者

定義 　a person who reads for pleasure

常用搭配語 　adj + reader

alert		眼尖的讀者
avid		閱讀狂
adult	reader	成人讀者
general		一般讀者
tabloid		八卦新聞讀者

實用例句

avid reader 書蟲

I am an avid reader and I am looking forward to the forthcoming *A Series of Unfortunate Events*.

我超愛看書的,我正在期待即將出版的波特萊爾大遇險。

alert reader 眼尖的讀者

Joe is an alert reader who enjoys gathering different errors from books he read.

Joe 是個眼尖的讀者,以從他閱讀過的書中收集不同的錯誤為榮。

Key Expression
情境表達套用語

kryptonite 致命傷 / 剋星

Poor writing has been my kryptonite when it comes to writing test.

只要遇到寫作測驗,差強人意的寫作一直是我的致命傷。

國家圖書館出版品預行編目資料

用搭配詞，英文變簡單／黃凱莉著 －－ 初版.
－－ 臺中市：晨星，2015.11
面； 公分. －－（Guide book；354）

ISBN 978-986-443-048-2（平裝）

1.英語學習 2.單字記憶

805.12　　　　　　　　　　104015264

Guide Book 354

用搭配詞，英文變簡單

作者	黃 凱 莉
編輯	林 宜 芬
封面設計	許 芷 婷
美術編輯	蔡 芠 倫
錄音	黃 凱 莉

創辦人	陳銘民
發行所	晨星出版有限公司
	台中市407工業區30路1號
	TEL：(04)23595820　FAX：(04)23550581
	E-mail：service@morningstar.com.tw
	http：//www.morningstar.com.tw
	行政院新聞局局版台業字第2500號
法律顧問	甘龍強律師
初版	西元2015年11月15日
郵政劃撥	22326758（晨星出版有限公司）
讀者服務專線	(04)23595819＃230
印刷	上好印刷股份有限公司

定價300元
（如書籍有缺頁或破損，請寄回更換）
ISBN 978-986-443-048-2

Published by Morning Star Publishing Inc.
Printed in Taiwan

◆ 讀 者 回 函 卡 ◆

以下資料或許太過繁瑣，但卻是我們了解您的唯一途徑
誠摯期待能與您在下一本書中相逢，讓我們一起從閱讀中尋找樂趣吧！

姓名：＿＿＿＿＿＿＿＿＿＿　性別：□ 男　□ 女　　生日：　　／　　／

教育程度：＿＿＿＿＿＿＿＿

職業：□ 學生　　　　□ 教師　　　　□ 內勤職員　　□ 家庭主婦
　　　□ SOHO族　　□ 企業主管　　□ 服務業　　　□ 製造業
　　　□ 醫藥護理　　□ 軍警　　　　□ 資訊業　　　□ 銷售業務
　　　□ 其他＿＿＿＿＿＿＿＿＿＿

E-mail：＿＿＿＿＿＿＿＿＿＿＿＿＿　聯絡電話：＿＿＿＿＿＿＿＿＿

聯絡地址：□□□＿＿＿＿＿＿＿＿＿＿＿＿＿＿＿＿＿＿＿＿

購買書名：用搭配詞，英文變簡單＿＿＿＿＿＿＿＿＿＿＿＿＿＿

・**本書中最吸引您的是哪一篇文章或哪一段話呢？**＿＿＿＿＿＿＿＿＿

・**誘使您 買此書的原因？**

□ 於 ＿＿＿＿＿ 書店尋找新知時　□ 看 ＿＿＿＿＿ 報時瞄到　□ 受海報或文案吸引
□ 翻閱 ＿＿＿＿＿ 雜誌時　□ 親朋好友拍胸脯保證　□ ＿＿＿＿＿ 電台DJ熱情推薦
□ 其他編輯萬萬想不到的過程：＿＿＿＿＿＿＿＿＿＿＿＿＿＿＿＿

・**對於本書的評分？**（請填代號：1. 很滿意 2. OK啦！ 3. 尚可 4. 需改進）

封面設計 ＿＿＿＿＿ 版面編排 ＿＿＿＿＿ 內容 ＿＿＿＿＿ 文／譯筆 ＿＿＿＿＿

・**美好的事物、聲音或影像都很吸引人，但究竟是怎樣的書最能吸引您呢？**

□ 價格殺紅眼的書　□ 內容符合需求　□ 贈品大碗又滿意　□ 我誓死效忠此作者
□ 晨星出版，必屬佳作！　□ 千里相逢，即是有緣　□ 其他原因，請務必告訴我們！

・**您與眾不同的閱讀品味，也請務必與我們分享：**

□ 哲學　　　□ 心理學　　□ 宗教　　　□ 自然生態　□ 流行趨勢　□ 醫療保健
□ 財經企管　□ 史地　　　□ 傳記　　　□ 文學　　　□ 散文　　　□ 原住民
□ 小說　　　□ 親子叢書　□ 休閒旅遊　□ 其他 ＿＿＿＿＿＿＿＿＿＿＿＿

以上問題想必耗去您不少心力，為免這份心血白費

請務必將此回函郵寄回本社，或傳真至（04）2359-7123，感謝！
若行有餘力，也請不吝賜教，好讓我們可以出版更多更好的書！

・**其他意見：**

晨星出版有限公司 編輯群，感謝您！

更方便的購書方式：

(1) 網　　站：http://www.morningstar.com.tw
(2) 郵政劃撥　帳號：22326758
　　　　　　　戶名：晨星出版有限公司
　　　　　　　請於通信欄中註明欲購買之書名及數量
(3) 電話訂購：如為大量團購可直接撥客服專線洽詢

◎ 如需詳細書目可上網查詢或來電索取。
◎ 客服專線：04-23595819#230　傳真：04-23597123
◎ 客戶信箱：service@morningstar.com.tw